VIETNAM TO SUNRISE

A Marine's Story of Love & War

BY CAPTAIN LES LEVY

VIETNAM TO SUNRISE: A Marine's Story of Love & War

Dedication

This novel is dedicated to the Marines of Kilo Company, 3rd Battalion, 1st Marines with whom I served during the Vietnam war era. While names have been changed, situations may seem very real and familiar to some. Nevertheless, this book is fiction. The Marines of Kilo 3/1 served bravely and honorably during this sad chapter in American history. To all my Marine brothers who survived, yet today still carry the physical and mental scars of battle, and to the families of our fallen brothers who paid with their lives in the pursuit of supporting American ideals in place at the time, you have my utmost respect and compassion.

Acknowledgements

Foremost I have to thank my beautiful wife, Judy, for accepting my decision to stay home on a five month sabbatical during the early 1990's when, while going through a mid-life crisis, I wrote the original manuscript for this book. After completing it, the old floppy discs and printed copies sat in a file drawer for almost eighteen years until about two years ago when my good friend Jack Watson, a retired airline captain, Vietnam army pilot and published author, encouraged me to dig it out of the drawer and work on it. I'm glad I did and I thank you, Jack. I also have to thank my editor, Nancy Quatrano, for her expertise in editing the book and for her tolerance in dealing with a "virgin author." Many thanks to Jackie Miller, my cover designer and formatting guru for her outstanding work, as well as Linda Hambright at Atlantic Publishing for her assistance and coordination to make this all happen.

CHAPTER 1

In Country, June 1968

From the air, all below seemed tranquil. Those aboard knew better. It was June 1968, just months after the deadly Tet offensive. The war was still going full bore. A small number of Marines aboard were returning for their second tour, but Lt. Elliot was here for his first tour. A "boot lieutenant" as some called the newly-minted second lieutenants fresh out of Quantico, he thought how he had just completed thirty-two of the most rigorous weeks of training imaginable. He felt prepared and ready even though he lacked combat experience. He also felt more than a little sick.

The turbulence was deep within his gut. Anxiously, he wondered if he would actually complete his thirteen-month tour of duty intact, or die here like so many others. The thought of going home in a body bag or perhaps on a medevac flight without any combination of his limbs was a reality.

His mind and heart rate began to race when he was jolted. He heard the screech of the tires on the runway and saw a wisp of blue smoke from beneath the plane. His head filled with the roar of the reversing thrust of the jet engines as the aircraft decelerated.

Would they even get off the plane alive? He'd heard rumors back in Quantico of planes bringing replacements just like this one being mortared upon landing. Marines trained to be combatants in war, killed before they ever got off the plane. With the sick feeling in his stomach passing, a tingling chill ran up his spine and he realized he was now in Vietnam... ready to do the job he was trained to do.

Max grabbed his carry-on bag and stood tall as he exited the plane and descended the ladder-way. At 6'2" and 205 lbs., he was in prime physical condition for his young twenty-two years, even better than his high school football years. With dark brown hair nearly shaven to the scalp, almost-black eyes set to each side of a perfectly sculptured nose, high cheekbones and a square jaw, all set upon broad shoulders, he looked the part of a Marine officer.

"All enlisted personnel E-5 and below fall in to your left" bellowed the staff sergeant. "Staff NCO's and above go with the Gunny. Officers report to the quonset building".

Max followed the small group to the designated building, dropped his gear and took a seat at a long table. They didn't wait alone long.

"Gentlemen, welcome to Nam," said a Marine who'd been around a while. The deeply tanned face was lined heavily across his forehead and his blue eyes were bloodshot. "I'm Captain Walker, and if you will each present your orders, we will get you transportation to your units as quickly as possible."

* * * * * *

Max climbed aboard the back of a six-by, a six-wheel drive, diesel powered vehicle and took a seat on the slatted green wooden bench along the side.

A young officer offered his hand. "Hi, I'm George Anderson." He grinned. "I guess we're here."

"Max Elliot, my pleasure. Yup, this must be the place, George".

As the truck rolled out of the airbase, Vietnamese civilians appeared in numbers. Once on the outskirts of the city, Max viewed shantytown. Row upon row of hopeless shacks constructed of plywood, cardboard and corrugated metal lined the road on either side. An old woman clad in what looked like black silk pajamas and a cone-shaped straw hat squatted by the doorway of one shack. Her deeply wrinkled face and black teeth made him cringe inside. She looked older than anyone he'd ever seen. As the truck rumbled past, Max met the woman's rheumy gaze.

"Betel nut," said Lt. Anderson. "Gives them a high and black teeth."

"I've heard about it," Max said. "Not very attractive."

Other women, dressed similarly to the old one, walked along the streets. Max observed a young girl, perhaps eighteen or nineteen, carrying vegetables in pans suspended by ropes from a pole carried across her shoulders. She was a pretty girl. She looked up as the truck slowly made its way through the narrow street and when she saw Max was looking at her, she quickly dropped her eyes to the ground, as if she were embarrassed.

A group of old men, also squatting, were arranged in a semicircle in front of a store, just another structure in a row of shacks. The men were smoking hand-rolled tobacco, probably containing betel nut, as they too had blackened teeth, separated by spaces where teeth once were.

"Stinks here, doesn't it," Max stated as he fought not to wrinkle his nose in disgust.

"Sure does. Probably the result of a lack of indoor plumbing," Anderson responded.

The six-by stopped momentarily to let some people move out of its path. Several Vietnamese on bicycles seemed to be taunting the driver, deliberately slow to move from the path of the heavy truck. A young man passed on the right driving a small lightweight Honda motorcycle. A group of young boys, perhaps eight to twelve years old stood watching the truck go by shouting recognizable English words- "hey Joe!" and "number one!" One boy, dressed in baggy shorts and a tattered t-shirt hollered "gimme chop-chop!"

As the truck once again began to roll, a baseball-size object thrown from among the boys landed in the bed of the truck. Frozen in horror, Max's immediate thought was—grenade! *Not this soon, I just got here!*

Another officer, a major sitting across from him, his back against the opposite side rail, didn't see the airborne object as it nicked his ear. The major jerked his head to the right as the rock landed with a harmless thud on the pile of duffel bags in the center of the truck bed. Max let out a shaky breath.

The major, touching his ear that apparently was not injured, asserted with trepidation, "I thought a sniper had me for a moment!"

"It was just a kid, Major," said Anderson.

"Kids here *kill* Marines, Lieutenant," the major replied.

Max and George exchanged a look but remained silent. The road began to open up some and the truck accelerated to 35 or 40mph. The smell of diesel fuel from the exhaust stacks of the six-by temporarily masked the other offensive odors.

After a long, bumpy and silent ride, the truck pulled through the entrance of the 1st Marine Division. The headquarters consisted of a consortium of small white buildings, hooch's and bunkers nestled on the side of a large hill that overlooked the sea. With its back against the hill, the compound seemed somewhat protected from incoming attacks, yet Max quickly realized that rockets or mortars launched with precision could land on Division turf.

******

The briefings at the Division level took two days. Lt. Elliot and the other officers, about twenty in all, were introduced to General Simpson, the Commanding General of the First Marine Division.

Subsequent briefings by staff officers from the intelligence section, known as G-2, and the operations section, or G-3, gave the officers an overall perspective of the enemy, sometimes referred to as the "illusive insurgent communist force." Max noted there was a lot of reference to "kicking ass and taking names". The G-4's briefing covered logistical support and everything from c-rations to tanks.

The personnel office pointed at Max. "Lt. Elliot, you're assigned to the Seventh Marines. They are currently operating southwest of here out of hill 55. And by the way..." The personnel officer was interrupted by his NCO.

"Sir, we just assigned Lt. Fowler to the 7th but the First Regiment needs platoon commanders badly."

The PO nodded. "Very well Sergeant. Assign the lieutenant to the First Regiment."

The personnel officer then looked at Max. "What I was about to say, Lieutenant, was that Captain Chuck Robb is the skipper of India 3/7. You may have been assigned to his company."

Max knew that Captain Robb was married to President Lyndon Johnson's daughter. The captain had told Max he'd met her in Washington while serving on a presidential detail at the White House.

"When do I join my unit, Sir?" Max asked.

"A jeep can take you over to Regiment in the morning. It's not that far."

Another series of briefings took place at the regimental level, stateside boots and utilities were packed in a duffel bag, to be replaced by jungle boots and jungle utilities. All necessary gear was issued including a U.S. Government Colt model 1911 .45 caliber automatic pistol and extra magazines and magazine pouches. Max was assigned to the Third Battalion.

The next day, heading further from the city of Danang, the small convoy arrived at the Third Battalion's makeshift headquarters. A few screen-enclosed, corrugated metal-roofed hooches, a command bunker, a semi-enclosed mess hall and some latrines, called "heads" in the Corps, comprised most of the base. Nailed to the front of one of the heads, a two holer, was a sign reading "library." There were a number of large tents erected in a row, their sides rolled up. Inside were lines of GI cots, some of them occupied by Marines either sleeping or reading. One man was cleaning his M-16 rifle.

It was the kind of heavy, wet heat that made you think you were breathing water. The dust on Max's body from the convoy ride ran in dark streaks down his cheeks and neck. The flak jacket and steel helmet only added to his discomfort. As he was about to leave the S-1's hooch, Max and Bob Larsen caught each other's eye.

"Bob, how the hell are you?" Max said as he strode toward his former classmate.

"Just fine, Max, I got here day before yesterday. Have you been assigned to a company yet?"

"Sure have. Kilo Company."

"Great, me, too! There's a resupply chopper heading out at 0600 tomorrow. I'm betting we'll both be on it."

Max nodded. "Hey, have you run into any of our other classmates?"

"Well, let's see," said Bob, rubbing his chin with the back of his dusty hand. I did see Franklin at Regiment. I think he went to Second Battalion. And I heard Hank Long is there also. How about you, you seen any of the guys?"

"Not here in country, but Bill Lindsey and I flew from Pendleton to Okinawa together. They should all be in country or enroute by now...there were forty-five of us headed this way."

"Yeah, that's right. The other guys are either in Pensacola for flight training or off training for artillery in Oklahoma—or tanks someplace else."

"You ever regret going into the grunts?" Max asked as they walked together.

"I don't know, sometimes maybe. Why, do you?"

Max thought deeply for a moment. "Nah, I don't, but I might if I hadn't watched all those John Wayne movies as a kid!"

They both laughed.

"Come on, I'll buy you a beer," Larsen said. "Could be a long time before we get another cold one."

* * * * * *

At the designated time, the CH-46 chopper was sitting on the pad as the two second lieutenants boarded. The door gunner, a corporal, looked like he had been in Nam awhile. He had that salty look. His utilities and boots were well worn. Instead of a steel helmet on his head he wore a camouflage soft cover.

His flak jacket was unzipped, and he grinned at the two rookie officers as he slowly and protrusively chewed his gum. Max couldn't see the corporal's eyes, because he wore dark sunglasses, but he interpreted the smirkish grin, as a warning about what lay ahead. Max figured he and Bob probably stuck out like virgins in a whore house with their new boots and uniforms. The jet engines on the helicopter revved up after the ammunition, cases of c-rations, mail and other supplies were loaded. Moments later, the bird was airborne.

As the helicopter gained altitude, the hot, humid air began to cool as if someone had turned on air conditioning. Without insulation, doors or windows, the noise from the rotors and engines made conversation impossible. Max sat across from the door gunner where he could look out at the country below, and chewed the inside of his cheek as anxiety began to take hold. He saw mostly green rice paddies and a brown river snaking its way through the valley. In the distance, mountains reached from the flat land below, all deep green, indicative of the thick jungle beneath the treetops. He was both awestruck by the beauty and frightful of what lie ahead. He wondered how many Viet Cong and NVA swarmed beneath that canopy. From the sound of what he'd heard in the past three days, there were too many to count. Surely he will soon find out firsthand.

They were headed for Thuong Duc, a small Vietnamese fishing village about thirty miles southwest, where Kilo was operating. According to the briefing by the major at Battalion there were no friendly forces between Kilo Company and the Laotian border, except for occasional reconnaissance inserts. The enemy, referred to as "Charley" passed through the narrow valley off the Ho Chi Minh trail, where it began to widen at Thuong Duc as it spread out towards Danang. It was a major infiltration route into Danang and it was Kilo Company's job to intercept the enemy.

Falling into somewhat of a trance from the whine of the engines coupled with the thud-thud sound of the rotor-blades as they sliced through the air, Max thought about last night, when having difficulty sleeping, he'd gone outside sometime after midnight.

Looking up at the brilliant starlit sky, he'd prayed. He didn't put much stock in any particular religion with all their pious hypocrisy, but he still believed in God. He believed in upholding the Ten Commandments and he believed in the golden rule. He didn't pray much, but when he did, he never asked God for anything for himself. Rather, he asked the good Lord to look after his family and others he loved.

But this time was different. Max thought how he prayed that God give him the strength—physically, mentally and emotionally—to lead his men into combat without anyone getting killed because he messed up. Also, for the first time in his memory, he asked God to look over him, to keep him alive. He desperately wanted to do his job well—but he also wanted to live.

CHAPTER 2

West Virginia University, 1967

As they flew deeper into enemy territory, Max drifted back in his mind to how he'd ended up in Vietnam.

The aging British motorcycle belched blue smoke from its exhaust as Max downshifted. The hills on the West Virginia University campus were very steep—so steeply inclined that they were paved with cobblestone rather than the usual asphalt. He could picture hot asphalt sliding down the hill before the appropriate equipment could roll it into place. About every eight or ten feet along the adjacent sidewalks, anywhere from three to six steps presented themselves to help ease the burden of ascending or descending the walkway. Downshifting was not only necessary to gain sufficient engine RPMs going up the hill, but necessary to use the engine to slow the bike on the way down.

It was the spring of 1967 and the cool, but warming air, felt much better upon his face than the stinging cold of the preceding winter. It was during the coldest months when Max had purchased the BSA Lightning. The former owner, a self-proclaimed motorcycle mechanic, professed he had rebuilt the engine. The untypical blue smoke, he assured, was only a temporary situation and the exhaust would become "barely detectable" once the piston rings "were set."

Max knew that by now the rings were set all right, set so just enough oil could pass by the rings to be burned in the combustion chamber, periodically fouling the spark plugs in the process. For this reason, Max always carried a small tool pouch, a piece of fine sandpaper and a rag with him on the bike to make the appropriate and frequent adjustments which were mandatory to avoid pushing the motorcycle home. Most British motorcycles only leaked oil. This one also burned it—profusely.

His medium length hair blew in the wind because helmets weren't required by law. Sunglasses kept his eyes from watering as the wind whistled by his face. A light blue work shirt, Levi's, and cordovan Bass Weejuns with no socks were his usual dress. A green windbreaker completed his attire. Other students seemed to seek more of the "preppy" look, but not only did Max not care for the look, but he couldn't afford to spend a lot of money on an expanded wardrobe. Keeping up with the seasonal wardrobes as presented in Playboy and GQ was beyond his interest as well as his wallet. It was all he had to afford the bike, and now he lacked funds to have it properly fixed, so it would just have to do. Having wheels at college, after three and a half years without any, took priority over new clothes.

About three-fourths of the way down the appropriately named "Hill Street," he made a U-turn in the road so he could park the bike facing uphill on the opposite side in front of the "Greeks," a small campus luncheonette owned and operated by two brothers who were Greek nationals, not Greeks as fraternity and sorority members were referred to.

"Hey Max, how's it going?" Lenny Albert shouted above the deep throaty sound of the still throbbing Lightning. He was just about to enter the freshly white painted wooden building along with two very good-looking coeds.

One he recognized as Lenny's girlfriend, Tammy, a very pretty sophomore with long brown hair and brown eyes. The other girl, slightly shorter than Tammy, he didn't know but was certain he'd like to. As she smiled at him, Max focused his eyes on her curves. He liked her long blond hair, blue eyes and enticing lips. It wasn't that he was particularly attracted to blondes but he liked what he was looking at.

"I'm just coming from psych class and thought I'd grab a bite before my next class," Max said.

"Great, so are we," said Lenny. "Let's get a table."

"Hi Tammy, good to see you," Max said.

"You too, Max. How's that statistics class coming?"

"Hard and boring. Why'd I ever take that course?" As he spoke, Max looked at the blond girl rather than Tammy.

"Oh, I'm sorry. Max, this is my roommate, Sally. Sally, this is Max Elliot, Lenny's fraternity brother."

"My pleasure, Sally."

"Nice to meet you too, Max."

"Where are you from, Sally?"

"Beckley, how about you?"

"Florida originally, but I went through high school in Jersey."

As they ate, the conversation remained trivial. He knew he wanted to see Sally again, so he asked her out for Friday night and she accepted. Following his last class of the day, he drove back to the Phi Sig frat house where he lived. He positioned the ten-foot board he kept hidden behind some shrubbery, revved the throttle and drove the motorcycle up the board which lay upon the steps onto the porch. Going up the board was the easy part...

stopping on the porch before hitting the front door required greater skill. As evidenced by the dents in the screen door, that skill had been developed over time. The trick was to lock the back wheel and spin the bike to the left upon landing. He did it with precision this time, perhaps because he felt good about his upcoming date with Sally Garfield.

After dinner, a number of frat brothers usually sat around in the TV room and watched the evening news, and then some game shows, followed by Star Trek. Max enjoyed the news. He sometimes studied a short while before coming back downstairs to watch Star Trek if he didn't have too much studying to do. He didn't like the game shows and wasn't a "Trekky," but it was something to do.

He was particularly interested in the news because of the war in Viet Nam. It was getting worse all the time and everyday they heard or read reports of Americans killed there. Police and the National Guard were being called to quell disturbances and demonstrations on college campuses and elsewhere around the country. Many radical groups professing peace were urging violence and anarchy. He could feel life changing around him, even on their remote campus.

West Virginia, in the heart of the "Bible belt", was not a particularly politically active campus. It was only recently that young men sported shoulder length hair, and marijuana was a new experience for many of his fellow students. As an athlete, Max didn't smoke anything, legal or otherwise.

The SDS—Students for a Democratic Society—was new on campus but it wasn't a faction Max was inclined to associate with. Many of its participants sat around in groups on lawns in front of college buildings, bearing peace signs and openly smoking pot. They were referred to as "hippies." Their dress was yet again different—tattered jeans and tie-dyed shirts over which hung beaded necklaces denoted their designation.

Volkswagens were the "vehicle de jour" of the hippies. One VW, an older model van, was painted in psychedelic colors. Whenever Max saw the van on campus it was jammed with occupants. It was like the van was their mascot and they remained with it whenever possible. But then Max began to realize that it was not so much the creative painting of the van, but the peace symbols superimposed on the psychedelics that were the real catalyst for their movement. Anti-establishment really meant anti-war.

Max knew a few of the people active in the movement. Allison, a junior drama major from Pittsburgh had played leading roles in University drama productions. . He'd met her during a drama class the previous semester. They dated briefly and enjoyed each other's company, but there was a different chemistry between them and their relationship never went beyond friendship. Allison opposed the war in Vietnam. Max was neither for it nor against it and he felt uncomfortable in no-man's land. It was then he decided to learn all he could about the war so he could take a position.

Friday evening finally arrived and he and Sally double dated with Lenny and Tammy, since Lenny had his mother's black '63 T-Bird—with red interior.

They went to the "Olympia," a college drinking establishment where the music was loud and the beer flowed freely. The beer in West Virginia contained 3.2% alcohol compared to 7% in neighboring Pennsylvania. Nevertheless, it was still intoxicating- as long as you drank enough and were at least eighteen.

After his third beer, Max yelled in Sally's ear. She nodded and they made their way to the ten by ten section of floor that served as the dance floor.

"Wow—you're really quite a dancer," Max said when they returned to the table.

"Well you're not too bad yourself, Max," she replied with a smile.

"Thanks, but you can probably dance like you do anytime. Me, I need a few beers to kind of loosen my inhibitions."

She laughed and he felt good inside. He slipped his arm around the back of her chair, sipped at his beer, and watched the others dance.

As the tune "Down Town" ended, Lenny and Tammy came off the dance floor and sat down.

"Anybody besides me hungry?" asked Lenny.

Tammy raised her hand and grinned. "Why don't we get a pizza?"

"Sounds good to me," said Max. "How about you, Sally?

"Great, let's go!"

Over the pizza, the conversation jumped from an upcoming "Letterman" concert, to hectic class schedules, to "what do you want to do when you graduate." Lenny was definitely set on going to law school in New England. Like Max, he was a senior and would graduate in June. Tammy and Sally, both sophomores, had plenty of time to decide, but at the moment, Tammy was a journalism major and Sally majored in sociology.

Max entered the conversation. "I'm thinking about going to grad school in industrial psych, but then again, I'd like a little break from school for awhile."

"You'll get drafted and go to Vietnam, that's the break you'll get," said Lenny.

"I heard they recently did away with graduate school deferments," said Tammy.

Max looked at his friend. "See, Lenny? I could be drafted right out of graduate school. In fact, you could be drafted out of law school as well."

"If that's the case, then maybe I'll have to think about law school in Canada," Lenny said facetiously.

"Did you guys see the sign someone put in front of the admin building today?" Sally asked.

"What sign was that?" Tammy asked.

It said, "New grading system" and continued below: "A, B, C, D, and V, for Vietnam."

Max sighed. It wasn't really a joking matter anymore. Thousands of Americans were being sent to—and dying in—Vietnam. The war was escalating, yet Max began to believe more and more in the government's objectives in South Vietnam. It didn't seem right to him that some Americans were dodging the draft. President Johnson was carrying on what the late President Kennedy had started, but it appeared that stopping the spread of communism made good sense.

As the evening came to a close, Lenny parked outside the girls' dorm and remained in the car a few minutes while Max walked Sally to the dorm. There were at least a dozen other couples in the area and it was just a few minutes before the midnight curfew. Men were not allowed in the girls' dorm, except in the lobby area when coming to pick up their date. There was a chill to the air, and in the dim light Max could see other couples embracing during their final moments together that evening. Max put his arms around Sally and brought her body closer to his.

"I had a good time tonight Max," she said.

"Hmm," he murmured. "I want to see you again."

"Me too," she replied. *"Hey, maybe you could help me study for my psych exam this week? We're learning all about Sigmund Freud. By the way, did you know that Freud was a Vietnamese physician?"*

"You do need to study, you dummy. Freud was a Viennese physician," Max said and they both laughed. With that, he gently kissed her, but only for a moment. With their lips still close he kissed her again, only this time he made it last. Sally put her arms around his neck and suddenly the chill in the air went unnoticed. There was warmth to the moment that he would think about until he drifted off to sleep.*

"See you later," he said.

"Good night, Max."

He turned and walked down the steps to the car. Lenny and Tammy were on their way up.

******

During the following week, a prominent CBS news correspondent was on campus to give a talk on the U.S. involvement in Southeast Asia. Max attended the lecture and listened carefully as the distinguished guest fielded a barrage of questions from the attendees.

Max raised his hand, then stood. "What would happen if we simply withdrew all American forces from Vietnam?"

"The communists would take over."

The blunt reply caught him in the chest like a fist. He was embarrassed to have asked such a stupid question, but what he really meant by the question was what would happen to the people of South Vietnam if the communists took over. He wondered if such an agrarian, third-world nation might not be better off if left alone, even if it meant communism. Another student thinking along the same channels posed the question better.

The speaker went on. "The Viet Cong continue and will continue to commit acts of violence against the citizens of South Vietnam. The guerrilla movement uses terror and death against all opposition. Any government official standing between it and its domination of rural areas is eliminated. In many instances, entire families and even entire villages have been massacred. Until they have won over the people psychologically and ideologically, many thousands of innocent civilians will die. And will Vietnam be the end of this spread of communism?" he asked, knowing very well the answer. "Of course not."

Max was crazy about Sally. Over the next several weeks they saw each other every chance they could and their relationship grew. On a gorgeous late April afternoon, he picked her up after they both were done with their classes for the day. Max knew she enjoyed riding the Lightning so long as it was moving.

What she did not like was stopping, as at a traffic light, when the fumes were like being on the wrong side of the road during a mosquito fogging. But on this day the fumes were to be left behind. One traffic light, two brief stop signs, and it was off campus and out onto the winding two lane mountain road twisting and turning, ascending and descending its way for twelve miles to Crystal Lake. It was the kind of road the machine was built for.

With all its current mechanical flaws, except for an occasional backfire, the bike gripped the pavement as its riders leaned in harmony in one direction and then the other as the ever-changing road ahead demanded. Max thought how he loved the thrill of the ride, almost mesmerized by the deep throaty sound of the engine and the smell of the fresh spring of the forest around them as it passed by in a blur.

He drove to their favorite spot by the lake. It was secluded and offered a grand view of almost the entire length of the nearly mile-long body of water. The lake was a deep mountain lake and even in June, diving in was like taking a polar plunge. Now, in April, it was cold enough to chill beer, but they would not be swimming. Surrounded entirely by forest, with the exception of a small resort on the shoreline where the lake turned, their spot was private. After spreading the blanket on the sprouting grass beneath the majestic oak, Max removed a large chunk of cheese, a knife, part of a loaf of French bread, and a flask of wine from the backpack bungeed to the chrome carrier.

"It's so beautiful here, Max. I just love it when we come here, don't you?"

"I just love being here with you," he said.

"Max, what's going to happen?"

"What do you mean, Sal?"

She nibbled at the bread, then at a sliver of cheese. "Well, in about another four weeks you'll be done with all your classes and exams and then you'll graduate."

Max finished eating a small piece of bread then looked at her and smiled. "That's right, I will."

"But what then? What will you do then? And what about us?"

"To tell you the truth, I'm not real sure. I don't mean about you— you know how much I care about you. It's just with this war going on in Vietnam, with the likely chance of being drafted, what are my choices?" Before she had a chance to answer, Max continued. "I could go to grad school and chance the draft. I could go to Canada and dodge the draft, or I could enlist."

"Would you want to go to Vietnam?" Sally said.

"Well, I really don't know. The more I watch the news or read the newspaper or listen to people speak, the more I believe in our objectives in Southeast Asia. And what would have happened to our country during World War I or World War II if most men refused to fight?" he asked. "If we don't stop the spread of communism today in Vietnam, can we be assured that our children will have the same freedoms we now have?"

Sally didn't say anything. Instead, she leaned toward him and kissed him.

The gentle wind whispered through the leaves above while the lake water lapped along the shoreline, and the soft sounds of passion emanated from the blanket placed between the water and the old motorcycle.

******

About twenty students sat around the tables in the student union, some eating or sipping soft drinks, while a few others seemed thoroughly engrossed in their studies. One table was vacant but had not yet been cleaned, and ketchup, French fries, and several empty paper cups littered it. Only two students were in the game room, involved in a lively game of ping-pong. The room to the left of the snack bar was much larger, comprising three fourths of the building. The Army representatives were the first to catch his eye as he entered. Each branch of the service had set up an eight-foot-long table and some metal folding chairs, all property of the university. They were lined up against the wall, had their respective marketing posters taped to the stark, concrete block wall behind them, and piles of brochures and pamphlets lined up like soldiers before them on the tables.

There were only a handful of students in the room. The Army representatives wore green uniforms adorned with lots of insignia. Max was not very knowledgeable about what they all meant, but they were impressive. One of the three soldiers wore highly polished black boots with his pants tucked above them and a green beret. Two large posters adorned the wall just behind him. One was of a tank coming over an embankment, its front end seemingly about to go airborne. Dirt flew everywhere, yet one could easily discern the driver, his helmeted head protruding from the area beneath the big gun in front of the turret. The other poster showed soldiers descending ropes from a helicopter that hovered above the ground. All in full battle dress with their rifles slung across their backs.

Max walked past the Army. Maybe because it was the Army that would draft him ultimately, or maybe because if he did go into the service and have to go to Vietnam, he was uncomfortable knowing he would be among mostly draftees who might not have the right attitude at a time his life might be dependent on his buddies around him.

He also walked by the Air Force table. He had taken two years of Air Force ROTC, but hadn't gone beyond the mandatory two-year requirement. The university was a "land grant institution" that meant all male students were required to take two years of either Army or Air Force ROTC. He had chosen the Air Force because he once thought he would like to fly, but towards the end of his sophomore year his 20/20 vision had worsened just enough to preclude qualifying for flight training and he didn't want to be a ground officer in the Air Force.

The destroyer crashing through the sea made for a really nice poster. The naval officer and the enlisted man with him were very cordial and helpful, but it seemed that the competition for Officer Training School in the Navy was great and the waiting list was now four to six months to get in if you were accepted. The rush to the Navy was obvious. Many a seasick-prone college graduate would rather be nauseated at sea than crawl through the jungles and rice paddies as the ground forces were sure to experience.

Two Marine Corps officers manned the last table. A first lieutenant and a captain, both in dress blues. The red stripe down the sides of their blue trousers, the black jackets and white hats covering almost shaven heads really made them stand out.

The emblem—the eagle, globe and anchor, was affixed on their hats as well as each side of the high collars of their jackets. A single poster presented itself on the wall behind the table. It did not depict tanks, helicopters or jet aircraft. There was no action to it at all. The poster showed the profile of a Marine second lieutenant in the dress blue uniform from the chin down, so the face remained anonymous. The rank insignia of a second lieutenant, the gold bar, was accentuated on the exposed epaulet of the uniform. Above where the head should have been was written: "Be a Leader of Men...Be a Marine Lieutenant." Max was impressed. Thoughts of outlandish masculinity and profuse pride raced through his mind. He began to visualize himself wearing the uniform. Can I do it?

The officers explained the program to him and advised that if he passed his physical examination he could report to Officer Candidate School at Quantico, Virginia, soon after graduation. There seemed such a heroic experience to be had in the Corps. His heart raced, but he knew what he had to do and he went for it. It was impulsive, yet concurrently exciting.

******

Eleven days later, Max drove the BSA north to Pittsburgh, Pennsylvania, an eighty mile trip that took about two hours considering the winding mountain roads in West Virginia and a fuel stop which included a spark plug de-fouling exercise as well. He arrived on time at the new federal building for his appointment for a physical examination.

Stripped to his undershorts, he was checked carefully by a team of doctors and medical technicians. He gave the usual body fluid specimens for lab analysis, did some aerobic exercises for which he was checked before and afterward and blew into a machine. At the conclusion, one of the examining physicians, a tall but lanky and serious looking man wearing black-rimmed glasses, approached him.

"Mr. Elliot?"

"Yes, Sir," Max replied.

"I'm afraid you fail to qualify, physically, for the Marine Corps program."

Max's heart sank. "What's wrong, Doc?" he asked.

The physician didn't look at him when he answered, but rather stared at the paper he held in his hand.

"Well, Mr. Elliot, you don't meet the qualifications in two areas. Number one, your vision, uncorrected, is just under the 20/40 limit; secondly, you have flat feet."

"But, Sir," Max explained, "My feet never hurt or bother me, and I recently got glasses for reading. I can see fine." Then Max added, "will that also disqualify me for the draft?"

The doctor's reply was quick.

"Oh no, you would pass an army induction physical."

"That's great," Max said. "I can serve in the Army but not the Marine Corps."

"Not true," the doctor said. "You could enlist in the Marines; you just don't qualify for OCS." He paused a moment before continuing. "Perhaps we can get you a waiver."

Max felt a thread of hope, as he had really geared himself for OCS, and every day for the past eleven days, he'd looked at that poster the recruiter gave him which now hung on the wall over his bed in the fraternity house.

"Wait here and I'll see what I can do," the doctor said.

Max anticipated a lengthy process whereby he would probably have to come back to Pittsburgh for further medical evaluation. The cafe style doors in the modern facility no sooner stopped swinging when the doctor walked back through them into the room where Max was told to wait. He wasn't gone more than ten seconds.

"Your waiver has been approved. Congratulations, Mr. Elliot." The physician showed Max the medical paper he held in his hand that contained the imprint of a large rubber stamp entitled: WAIVER.

Over the next several days, Max bore the brunt of jokes and teasing comments by his fraternity brothers over his decision to join the Marine Corps. Another brother, Art Adams, was also a graduating senior and going into the military. Art, however, completed four years of Air Force ROTC and was going into some non-flying capacity. Whether he would ever see action in Vietnam was less likely than the almost assured position Max was in. It became commonplace for one or more to break out in the first few lines of the Marine Corps Hymn whenever Max walked into the frat house.

"From the halls of Montezuma, to the shores of Tripoli..." began to sound better and better to him. He was proud to have joined and looking forward to graduation and his orders to report to Quantico.

Someone yelled up the stairs. "Max, the phone's for you. It's Sally." He hadn't heard the phone ring as he was studying for finals. He took the steps two at a time and grabbed the phone.

"Hey, Sal. What's up?"

"I'm lonely, Max."

"Aren't you supposed to be studying?" he asked.

"I am, but I haven't seen you in three days. Let's take a study break and go down to the Greeks for coffee."

Max thought briefly. "Okay, I'll pick you up in fifteen minutes. See ya then."

******

"Okay Sal, you got me out here, now you're not talking. What's wrong?"

She stirred her coffee, but didn't look at him. "Are you going to Vietnam, Max?""Probably," he answered.

"But you could be killed!"

"Sally, we talked about this before. It's what I have to do. Faced with choices, this is the one I chose. Someone has got to do it."

"But why you?" she asked, her eyes filled with tears.

"But why not me?" he answered. "I also have to prove to myself I have what it takes to become an officer in the Marine Corps. It's become a personal challenge for me—besides my belief in serving my country."

"But it won't be the same without you here," she said. "I'm really going to miss you, not to mention worry about you."

"Look Sal, I've still got to go through OCS in Quantico. It could be a year before I go to Vietnam. Besides, Quantico, Virginia, isn't all that far from here. We'll see each other."

They left their coffees almost untouched and left in silence.

He drove her back to the dorm, set the kickstand on the motorcycle but did not get off when Sally did. He threw his leg over the seat and sat there. He put his arms around her and pulled her gently towards him. He looked into her eyes which closed as her lips touched his.

She slowly pushed herself away, looked sadly into his eyes, then turned and walked away. He watched her climb the stairs and enter the dorm.

He no longer felt like studying. The night air was cool but felt good. Max was troubled. He didn't drive back to the frat house. Instead he turned the Lightning up the hill and out of town to the Richland Cafe, a small bar three or four miles out of town. They served beer on tap in huge twenty-four-ounce frosted goblets. He drank two.

******

Graduation came and went. Max and Sally said their goodbyes, among her tears. He assured her he would see her again, but stoically told her he wanted her to date other men while he was away. There was no need for her not to when she had two more years of college. Reluctantly, she agreed.

Max had his orders from Headquarters, United States Marine Corps. He was given a date to report to Officer Candidate School, Quantico, Virginia.

There was no turning back.

CHAPTER 3

Thuong Duc, June 1968

The CH-46 chopper flew high over Thuong Duc before spiraling downward towards a small knoll connected by a saddle to the main hill. During the descent, Max observed Marines meandering about. A trench followed the uneven terrain forming the perimeter of the encampment upon the hill and sandbags formed a small berm along its outer edge. Intermittently along the trench were bunkers, some with sandbagged roofs, others completely open. He could see artillery pieces that looked like 105's and some 81mm mortars. In the center of the hill, at what appeared to be its highest point of elevation and out in the open, a Marine sat on a large wooden box. His utility trousers were down around his ankles over his boots. He continued to go about his business while shielding his eyes from the dust created as the chopper set down nearby.

"Let's move it!" the crew chief shouted as he threw a mailbag, ammunition, and cases of c-rations out the door. The pilot kept the engines turning, ready to take off in an instant should he come under fire. Several

Marines from Kilo Company were on hand to retrieve the supplies after which the chopper would once again be airborne.

"Come on Max, I think this is home sweet home," said Lt. Bob Larsen.

"Let's go meet the skipper," Max said, as he and Larsen jumped from the helicopter.

About half way up the saddle the two lieutenants stopped in their tracks.

"Well, well, looky what we got here," said the sergeant with a grin from ear to ear.

"I'll be damned," Max said. "Sgt. Gorman, how the hell are you?"

"Hello, Sgt. Gorman," said Bob as he extended his hand.

Gorman was one of the Quantico drill instructors responsible for molding Max and Bob's OCS class into Marines. He was tough and spared no compassion when it came to mental and physical harassment.

An E-5 and career Marine, Sgt. Gorman was really squared away. He was black, of medium build, and solid as a rock cliff. Max recalled a thousand extra pushups in OCS, all ordered by Sgt. Gorman when Max was caught laughing at the NCO's harassment. Keeping a sense of humor was important in OCS for survival. Those candidates who took insults to their family and person to heart, and succumbed to other psychological harassment, had a real difficult time. As many as forty-to-sixty percent of each class never made it to commissioning and had to serve two years as enlisted.

Now, here in Vietnam, six months later, the two former candidates stood before Sgt. Gorman once again, only now they were commissioned officers and out ranked him.

"Gentlemen, I heard we was to get us a couple of brand new lieutenants," Sgt. Gorman said. "Let me introduce you to the company commander."

Near the top and center of the hill and not far from the "one-holer," was a small tent surrounded by sandbags arranged to about four feet high. It sported a narrow opening on one side for entry, in front of which was another row of sandbags to prevent shrapnel from entering the front door.

"Captain Newbury, those new officers are here," said Gorman.

"How do you do Sir, I'm Lt. Max Elliot."

"And I'm Lt. Bob Larsen."

Without sparing them more than a glance, the commander addressed them. "Elliot, you'll take command of the first platoon," he said. "Larsen, you have the second platoon. You can both introduce yourselves to Lt. Cullen who has the third platoon." The captain continued in his brusque, unfriendly manner. "Lt. Elliot, Sgt. Gorman is your platoon sergeant."

"Uh, Captain," began Max, "Sgt. Gorman was my drill instructor in Quantico and I think it best if..."

"If nothing, Lieutenant!" the captain blurted. "Sgt. Gorman, go introduce the lieutenant here to his platoon. Oh, and by the way Lieutenant, be ready to take your platoon out on patrol in two hours."

Max glared at the captain who stood about six feet tall, was thin with narrow shoulders and a dark bushy mustache.

"Yes, Sir," he said slowly and emphatically as he turned and exited the tent. "Is he always this friendly, Sarge?"

"Actually Lieutenant, he's an asshole. The troops don't like him either. They have a six-hundred-dollar price on his head."

"No shit!" Max exclaimed. "You mean he might get zapped by someone in his own company?"

"Could very well happen. I just hope I don't see it and have to testify against one of the men."

"Besides his pleasant personality," Max questioned, "what is it they dislike about him enough to snuff him?"

Sgt. Gorman pointed off to the north. "See those mountains over there on the other side of the rice paddies?"

"Yeah."

"See those mountains to our immediate west?" again he pointed.

"Yes, I do."

The sergeant now pointed to the south. "See those mountains to our south, just across the river?"

"What's your point, Sarge?"

"My point, Lieutenant, is that the VC are *all* over these mountains. There are also recon reports of an NVA division out there somewhere. The captain is supposed to be running company size patrols out of here and the troops know it. Instead, he runs platoon patrols and he keeps his ass here on this hill, always with at least one platoon to protect him. He ain't been off this hill since we got here two weeks ago."

"So if one of the platoons should run into a VC company or worse yet, an NVA division, it would be in deep shit," Max replied, making more of a statement than a question.

"You got the picture, Lieutenant."

Max and Sgt. Gorman now reached the area of the first platoon. The men were spread out over an area along the perimeter. Although no one was actually in the trench, a few were sitting along the edge. Two men seemed engaged in conversation while another appeared to be writing a letter.

Just a few meters behind the trench, Max observed a makeshift tent consisting of a couple of ponchos supported by poles. Within, a man lay sleeping. Next to the tent was another makeshift shelter.

This one was constructed of sandbags arranged to about four and one half feet high on four sides except for the front that bore the addition of an entranceway consisting of a semicircle piece of steel culvert about two feet high, under which one would crawl to gain access to the interior. The bunker also contained a poncho-covered roof supported by an assortment of scrap wood and a few pieces of metal, but hardly anything substantial enough to support the weight of sandbags. Without a sandbagged roof, protection was limited to an enemy mortar or artillery round landing outside and not within the structure. With the addition of the culvert and sandbags protruding from its front, the structure bore a resemblance to an Eskimo igloo—the sandbags resembling blocks of ice.

About three-dozen Marines idled about the area. Some were reading magazines or paperbacks, while others were cleaning weapons or not doing much of anything. They looked like seasoned veterans of the war. Military dress codes were relaxed in combat. All the men wore jungle boots and green jungle utility trousers, but from the waist up was an array of dress, some bare-chested, others wearing only their flak jacket. Still others wore just green T-shirts or their utility jacket, flak jackets optional, something Max would change, making them mandatory. A number of men had government issued green towels strung over their necks. Headgear ranged from none to camo-covered steel helmets, along with several styles of military-issued soft covers.

As he walked among the men, Max sensed all eyes upon him. His gold bars glistened in the bright hot sun and his uniform and equipment were new, further drawing their attention.

"Sgt. Gorman, assemble the platoon," he ordered. "I want to meet the men."

"Now Lieutenant?" questioned the sergeant.

"Right now, Sergeant Gorman."

"On your feet, Marines!" shouted Gorman. "Corporal Tanner, Corporal Barfield, Corporal Garrison, get your squads over here ASAP! Sergeant Ualena, get Shane and the Doc—on the double!" Within a minute, the 1st platoon of Kilo Company stood, or sat, about.

"Men," Max began, "I'm Lieutenant Elliot, your new platoon commander." As he spoke, a muffled laugh emerged from the midst of the platoon. He ignored it and went on. "You see who I am, but you will no longer see me wearing these bars." He removed the gold bars from his collar and placed them in his pocket. It was foolish to wear the rank insignia of an officer and stand out among the men as their leader. Especially since the enemy's first choice of target would be the platoon commander, followed by the radio operator.

"In short time, I look forward to getting to know all of you but the skipper has advised me we go on patrol within two hours, so get your gear ready. I'll get the patrol order and pass it on to the squad leaders shortly. That's all for now, but I want the squad leaders to remain. Oh, and by the way, I don't want anyone saluting me when we're out here in the bush, for the same reason I no longer wear my rank insignia. Dismissed."

"Welcome Lieutenant, I'm Sgt. Ualena, platoon guide."

"My pleasure, Sgt. Ualena. Where are you from?"

"Hawaii, Sir."

Sgt. Ualena had all the features of a Hawaiian- dark hair, eyes and skin. Max had never been to Hawaii except for the one-hour refueling stop on his way from California to Okinawa during which time he was allowed to exit the plane and walk around inside the terminal.

"Corporal Barfield here, Lieutenant."

"Which is your squad, Corporal?" Max asked.

"Second, Sir."

Sergeant Gorman then interjected. "Lieutenant, this is Corporal Garrison, third squad, and Corporal Tanner, first squad."

"I'm pleased to meet you all," Max stated. "I'm sure we'll all work well together."

"Same here, Lieutenant," said Cpl. Barfield.

Two other men sat nearby observing the exchanges of pleasantry. They were leaning back against some sandbags. Max hadn't met them yet.

"Who do we have here?" Max questioned.

"Get on your feet and come meet the lieutenant," Sgt Gorman said to the two. Following his command they slowly got up and ambled across the few meters to where Max stood.

The first to speak was a good-looking, young lance corporal with sandy brown hair and a big friendly smile. "Hi Lieutenant, I'm Lance Corporal Shane, your radio operator. Welcome to Nam."

"Thank you, Corporal Shane. Should I say it's a pleasure to be here?"

"Whatever, Lieutenant. It's the only war we got…you just got to love it!"

"So I'm told," Max replied.

The red haired man next to Shane wore dark sunglasses. His utility jacket was unbuttoned exposing his dog tags, a cross on a separate chain and a "John Wayne tool," hanging from his neck. The latter tool being a small metal object used to open cans of c-rations and suspended from the same chain as his dogtags. The military designated it a P-38. He had a rounded face, a ruddy complexion and more than his fair share of freckles. He held a can of beer.

"How's the beer?" Max asked as he looked directly at the man, not able to see his eyes hidden behind the dark glasses.

"Warm as piss, but wet," came the reply.

From the black metal chevrons on his collar, Max knew this was a navy hospitalman, otherwise known as a corpsman. They were assigned to the Marines and provided indispensible medical treatment for the wounded.

"Do you have a name?" Max asked.

"Shepherd, but most guys just call me 'Doc.'"

"Okay, Doc, I hope you're sober enough to go on patrol."

"No problem, Lieutenant." Doc Shepherd turned and walked away.

"Sgt. Gorman, how long have you been running the platoon?" Max asked. "What I mean is, how long since the last lieutenant left?"

"Going on near a month now I suppose. We were operating up north when he got hit."

"How bad?"

"Pretty bad, Lieutenant. We flew him out on an emergency evac. He took a round in his chest. I don't even know if he made it."

"Was he a good platoon commander?"

"He might have been, but it would be hard for me to say. He only lasted three days with us."

"Well Sgt. Gorman, I'll just have to try and beat my predecessor's longevity record."

"I hope you do, Lieutenant."

"Listen Sarge, are you going to have a problem with me being your platoon commander?

"Not a bit. Besides, I know you're in shape because I made you do about a million pushups in OCS!"

"That you did," Max said as the two men smiled at one another. "I'll go see the skipper now and get our patrol order."

At Captain Newbury's tent, Max hesitated momentarily before entering. "You have a patrol order for me, Captain?"

Newbury had been writing a letter when Max entered the tent. Putting the letter aside, the captain stood and pointed to a map of the area he had affixed to a piece of plywood.

"You are here. You will conduct a platoon-size patrol of *this* area." As he spoke, the captain used a pointer he had apparently carved from a stick to point out specific areas on the map. "You will thoroughly search out this village here, Chan Son. I'll be on frequency 60.35. I want you off this hill by 0900 and back before dark. Any questions?"

"Just one," Max said.

"That's just one, *Sir*," came the reply, long and slow with emphasis on the word "sir".

Max could feel his blood pressure rise. "Just one, Sir," Max repeated, but slowly and deliberately this time. "What is my mission exactly, Sir?"

"Your mission, Lieutenant, is to seek out and destroy the enemy. Did they forget to teach you that in Quantico?"

"No, Sir."

"That will be all, Lieutenant."

Back at the platoon's location, Sgt. Gorman had things under control. The men appeared nearly ready to move out. "Day patrol, right?" said the sergeant.

"That's right. Let's take one meal per man. Do we have plenty of ammo and flares, Sarge?"

"We're all set, Lieutenant. Do you want to take the machineguns?

"Yeah, let's take them. How many men do we have?"

"Sergeant Ualena can tell you exactly. Sgt. Ualena," Gorman called out, "What's our head count?"

"In the field, we have thirty-four enlisted, one navy and one officer. We have nine men either on R&R or at BAS."

BAS was the Battalion Aid Station, where men were sent for minor wounds or sickness. Malaria was a frequent problem in Nam even though the corpsman gave out malaria pills every Sunday. Max had seen a number of Marines running extremely high fevers alternated with chills when he was at Battalion. They had malaria.

Including the attached weapons section, which consisted of two M-60 machineguns and one 60mm mortar, a full complement of men for a rifle platoon should be fifty-four. The first platoon was going on patrol with thirty-six men including himself.

Max assembled his squad leaders along with Sgt. Gorman, Sgt. Ualena, Cpl. Shane, and Doc Shepherd. He issued his patrol order along with the appropriate signals to be used and check points to be passed.

Finally, he advised all that it was 0840. They would move out at 0845.

CHAPTER 4

New South Wales, Australia

On September 28, 1949, George McEwen and his wife Delia, celebrated the birth of their second child, a girl they named Amber Dawn McEwen. The family prospered as ranchers, raising mostly beef cattle. Amber grew up a tomboy, shadowing her older brother, John, whenever he didn't shoo her off. She learned to ride a horse at such an early age that equitation was as natural to her as walking.

In January 1967, summertime in Australia, Amber met a jackaroo named Gordon Hamilton who was hired on by John, who served as head stockman on the ranch. A jackaroo is a ranch hand who becomes a stockman after so many years. Gordon had been a stockman on another spread up in Queensland for eight years prior to coming to work for the McEwen's, but had to prove himself first as a jackaroo before earning stockman wages.

Amber was seventeen. She was 5'6" tall with as shapely a body as any woman would envy and any man desire. Voted the prettiest girl in her class, her long straight brunette hair framed a face blessed with eyes as green as a tropical sea. Her beauty was natural and she radiated that wholesome outdoorsy look that made her the stuff boys dream about. She was also a daddy's girl and her father's pride.

"I'm going to ride down to the river to check on those new calves," Gordon said. "Want to ride along, Amber?"

"I don't think so Gordon, I told mother I would help her in the garden this afternoon."

"Oh, come on girl, you know you would rather ride than pull weeds. Besides, we won't be long. I have to get those bullocks to the chutes yet before sundown."

"All right then, but we ride back direct after checking the calves," she said. "Deal?"

"You drive a hard bargain girl, but I accept your deal."

"I'll saddle Tuffy and be right along."

The McEwen ranch was named "Sunrise." It was situated just west of the eastern highlands, that fertile land region that extends along the east coast of the continent from northern Queensland to Tasmania. Lush green mountains rose on the horizon in the east while the beginnings of the grasslands spread to the west. Tributaries of the Murray River gracefully wound through some of Sunrise's twenty-five hundred acres.

Gordon was eleven years Amber's senior. He was tall, muscular, handsome and self-confident. Too much so, according to the girls in Heathcote who saw him as cocky and arrogant and a man who was reluctant to take no for an answer while taking liberties with the ladies. No one really knew much about him. All anyone knew, including the

McEwens, was that he came from Queensland, had a captivating smile, and was a good stockman.

The two riders covered the distance to the river at a slow canter in about half an hour. Nearly one-hundred-twenty calves roamed close to their mothers' side as yet other cows, heavy around the middle, stood ready to drop calves of their own.

"Let's give our mounts a breather," Gordon said as he dismounted.

"Come on Gordon, you said we would head right back," Amber protested.

"We'll just be a minute. Give that animal of yours a drink and a chance to cool down some."

"Okay, but just for a moment." Amber stepped down from her horse and before her left foot slipped from the stirrup iron, Gordon was behind her with his arms reaching around her waist. She turned, now standing with Tuffy against her back and Gordon's face close to hers.

"Now Gordon, seems you had more on your mind than checking calves," she said. Amber was attracted to Gordon yet intimidated by his forwardness and the fact he was twenty-eight years of age and considerably more experienced with girls than she with men.

"You know I'm crazy about you, don't you?"

"Gordon, I think we better be going," she said as she slid her hands to his chest and began to push herself away.

"All right, but now that I got you where you can't get away, tell me you will go with me to the dance Saturday night."

"I don't think my father would approve of that," she said.

"And why not? Am I not good enough for a McEwen?"

"It's not that, Gordon. You're just, well… just, just, older. And besides, John says you've told some pretty good stories about your experiences with the ladies in Queensland. I don't think father would approve of his innocent little Amber keeping company with such a ladies man."

"Innocent you say? Why, what was it I heard about you and that Donor bloke having a little roll in the hay after the last muster?"

"Who told you about that?" she exclaimed with a red face.

"Never mind that, just ask your father. Okay? Just ask him. Fair enough?"

Both frightened and excited, Amber agreed. "I'll ask him. Can we go now?"

"Sure. Just one more thing." With that, Gordon pressed his lips to hers. Without protest she could not deny to herself she was enjoying it. In a moment as he held her tighter, she moved her arms around his neck.

The following day as John was saddling his horse in the barn, Amber received a dose of sibling advice. "Listen, it's not that I dislike Gordon. Actually, I enjoy being around him and going to the pub and downing a few beers now and then, but he's not right for you. I have a gut feeling that there is something ominous about him. I just can't figure it out yet. Why don't you go to the dance with Jeremy Donor? He's only asked you a hundred times," John said.

"Because I don't *want* to go to the dance with Jeremy Donor, that's why!" she protested. "Gordon is really quite nice and certainly earns his wages on Sunrise. You just told me you like him" she said. "I do like Gordon; I just don't want him courting my sister, that's all."

"John, you're impossible! Anyway, I'm woman enough to decide for myself whose company I shall keep!" Amber sneered and strutted from the barn.

Escorted to the community center that Saturday night by Jeremy Donor, Amber divided her time between Jeremy and Gordon Hamilton, much to the dislike of Jeremy. But Jeremy, a classmate of Amber's, and son of a neighboring rancher, was no match to Gordon with his smooth talking charm.

"She's here with me, mate!" Jeremy voiced with anger after Gordon again cut in on a dance.

"She's here to have a good time, that's all, and you were just lucky enough to escort her here," Gordon said. "Now why don't you get yourself a lemonade and let us finish this dance."

Amber intervened as the tempers began to erupt. "Now boys, why don't we all get some lemonade? Besides, I'm hungry." She diffused the moment none too soon.

Tactfully, Amber spent the remainder of the evening with Jeremy, paying close attention to him, much to his pleasure. Meanwhile, Gordon continued to down more than enough Foster brews and danced with all the other pretty girls, all the while keeping an eye on Amber.

Towards the end of the dance, Amber faked a yawn. "I've had a wonderful time tonight, Jeremy, but I'm really getting tired now and I have to get up before dawn to help John with the muster."

"I'll take you home, then," Jeremy said.

"Listen, Jeremy, it's really quite out of your way to drop me at Sunrise,

I'll just catch a ride back with Gordon. He has a busy day ahead tomorrow also, and I don't want father to be paying wages to a jackaroo that's too drunk or too tired to earn his keep. I think he has had enough partying for one night."

"Nah, it isn't much out of the way. I'd much prefer I drive you home."

Amber softly kissed Jeremy then looked into his eyes with those captivating green irises of hers. "Really, you don't have to be jealous of every jackaroo on Sunrise. Now I'll be going home straight away with Gordon. You be sure to call on me, okay?"

Like a wounded puppy, Jeremy consented, much to his disappointment. "I'll call you tomorrow."

"Goodnight Jeremy, and thanks for a wonderful time." With another kiss, this one not more than a quick peck, Amber turned and went over to Gordon who was leaning on the bar, carousing with several girls while concurrently downing another Fosters.

"If you're sober enough, Mr. Hamilton, I would appreciate a lift back to Sunrise."

"Ah, ladies, I regret I must take leave. The boss's daughter is in distress and being the devoted stockman I am, I must oblige." The other girls giggled but Amber was annoyed.

"Cut the crap Hamilton. Are you escorting me home or shall I request Jeremy do so?"

Now standing erect, Gordon tipped his felt jackaroo hat. "Shall we depart now, my lady?"

With that, Amber exited the dance hall with Gordon close behind. John McEwen watched them leave together from his position at the opposite end of the bar. He also saw Jeremy Donor with a shunned expression watch them leave. John didn't try to stop them, but was obviously disturbed.

"You wouldn't have started a fight with Jeremy, would you?" she asked as the pickup moved along the narrow road.

"Nah, I just would have finished it if that wet-nosed kid had started it."

"Why did you leave Queensland, Gordon?"

"It was just time, that's all. Besides, I heard the most beautiful girl on the entire continent was somewhere in New South Wales on a spread called Sunrise. I just had to see for myself."

"And?" Amber queried.

"It was a ruse," he jokingly said. "She had the face of a boar-hog."

Amber jutted her elbow hard into Gordon's ribcage.

"Ow! Can't take a little jesting, can you?"

At a side road a few miles before Sunrise, Gordon turned onto the dirt road and parked a few hundred meters down. After turning off the engine, the only sounds that could be heard through the open windows on that warm night were the sounds of the crickets chirping their love songs. Amber could hear herself breathing deeply and rhythmically as Gordon reached his arm around her shoulder and smoothly pulled her towards him as their lips met. She surrendered her emotions, allowing the suave and macho stockman to take greater liberties with her body than she had ever let Jeremy Donor or any other man.

"I saw you leave the dance with Hamilton last night," John said to Amber the next day as they rode to the south pasture to round up some calves for branding.

"He just drove me home, that's all."

"He's no good for you, Amber. Won't you listen to me?"

"I'll do as I please, and you can stay out of my personal life if you will!" With that, she spurred Tuffy and galloped ahead.

That evening, John had a talk with his father about Amber. "He's a good hand, but I don't want him having anything to do with Amber," John said.

George McEwen responded as a father who trusted his daughter unequivocally. "John, it's good you look after your sister as you do, but I'm sure if anything, it's just a teenage crush she has on Gordon. It will pass, just like all the other crushes she's had on boys. As soon as he starts paying too much attention to her, the challenge will be gone and she'll tell him to go kiss a ewe."

"I hope so," John said, "but I think I will have a chat with Mr. Hamilton."

"He's a good hand, John, don't run him off just yet."

"I won't, Father, I'm just going to have a talk, that's all."

The next day was hot, very hot, and the sweat mixed with the dust as the hard working stockman mustered the calves into the paddock for branding. John wasn't quite sure how he was going to approach Gordon about his sister, but during a brief rest period as they scooped water from the bucket, John asked: "Gordon, it appears you've got an eye for my sister."

"Now what gives you that notion, John?"

"I've seen how you look at her, and I saw you two leave the dance together."

"It's nothing, really John, don't be bothered by it."

"I hope you're right, Gordon. You're a dang good stockman and the Sunrise needs men like you, but I would prefer you leave Amber alone. She's just a kid." John put down the ladle and went back to work.

Weeks passed, and Amber secretly rendezvoused with Gordon, each meeting plunging her deeper into an infatuation and deeper under his control. She was a strong willed girl, but Gordon had a captivating rein on her.

John maintained his suspicions all along, but never knew for certain about the encounters occurring between Amber and Gordon. Gordon continued to work well for the ranch. In fact, he was one of the hardest working stockman on the ranch, spending the biggest part of his life in the saddle, daylight till dark, six and sometimes seven days a week.

CHAPTER 5

On Patrol

The first platoon of Kilo Company walked down the east face of the hill that overlooked the small fishing village of Thuong Duc. South of the hill, small wooden boats lay along the shoreline of the Song Vu Gia River. On this patrol, the first for Lt. Max Elliot, he would not make contact with the people of the village.

Max ordered his platoon to stagger and spread out ten meters between men as they reached the dirt road in the valley below. The patrol route would take them northeast about eight hundred meters, across a wooden bridge that transversed the Song Con, and then north and northeast along the east bank of the river as it spiraled through the surrounding rice paddies. At a point about fifteen hundred meters upstream, the river turned sharply to the west.

On the map a trail depicted along the patrol route forked with one branch heading north into the mountains only three hundred meters beyond. Max designated this juncture as Checkpoint Alpha.

Where the trail continued west, the map showed another village, Tai Son—about one thousand meters, or a "click" as the Marines called it—to the northwest. Beyond, as the valley narrowed in its geographical journey northwesterly, were seven other villages or hamlets ending with An Diem, six clicks away, where the valley met the mountains.

Kilo One would not venture nearly so far today. The patrol moved on without incident. It was not the rainy season and most of the rice paddies were dry or contained only so much water as to cover the lower half of the Marines' boots.

Max kept his platoon off the trail, which likely was booby-trapped in hopes of surprising an unsuspecting victim. Staggered and spread out, Max thought how *his* platoon represented a formidable threat to the enemy. He felt powerful and in command.

As he sloshed through the paddy, he watched a small water snake slither out of his path. He carefully stepped up and over the paddy dike. The water squished from the tiny drain holes on the arch side of each boot. He stepped down again into the next paddy, this one not so wet.

Max concentrated on the job at hand. Bravo squad, the second, had the point, followed by Alpha and then Charlie in the rear. The platoon CP, consisting of himself, Sgt. Gorman, Sgt. Ualena, Cpl Shane and Doc Shepherd moved between Bravo and Alpha. No one talked and all seemed alert. Occasionally he heard some static overriding the squelch on the radio.

Cpl. Shane always shadowed his platoon commander, but still maintained his ten-meter distance.

"Kilo One Actual, Kilo One Actual, Kilo One Bravo." The voice on the radio spoke quickly but not loudly. Kilo One Actual was Max's radio call sign. Cpl. Shane quickly acknowledged.

"Kilo One Bravo, this is Kilo One, go."

"Advise Kilo One Actual we are at Checkpoint Alpha."

"Roger Bravo, will advise. Standby."

"Tell Bravo to cross the river at the sandbar, move one hundred meters west and get down in position," Max ordered. Cpl. Shane relayed the command to Bravo.

As Max forded the chest-high water, holding his now un-holstered .45 in the air, he wondered what he would encounter in the village of Chan Son just a couple of hundred meters ahead of Bravo's position. All the villages in this area had been resettled, moving civilians to resettlement areas nearer Danang. Generally, any people still remaining were wives, children or other family members of the Viet Cong. If not, they were Viet Cong sympathizers or members of the Viet Cong infrastructure. Besides women and children, Max was told he would only see old men in these villages. The older boys and young men were Viet Cong. They mostly stayed in the mountains by day and stealthily returned to their villages by nightfall.

Approximately two thirds of the way across the river, a voice in somewhat of a drawl called out from behind him. "Hey Lieutenant, there's a snake coming down the river, can I shoot it?"

While it was daylight, Max didn't want to make his presence in the area any more obvious than he had to. Certainly, firing a shot now might awaken or alert the enemy. Without looking back, he simply said, "No."

"But Lieutenant, it's a big snake and it's gonna bite me."

This time the request was spoken with considerably more concern. Max, now a little annoyed at the re-iterance of the Marine's request turned in the water in time to see the largest waterborne serpent he had ever seen.

The venomous creature had its mouth open, presenting a pair of fangs armed in anticipation of sinking themselves into the flesh of the human now only a few meters downstream.

"Shoot that son of a bitch!" Max exclaimed. From the M-16 came a burst of automatic fire. The six-foot long venomous creature was lifted from the water. In a second, it returned from whence it came, contorted and segmented. Max looked into the eyes of the tall slender dark haired Marine who was returning the look. Max nodded and the man nodded back. Max turned to complete the river crossing.

When the entire platoon was on shore on the west side of the Song Con, Max positioned the three squads on line and gave the order to sweep the village. Among the thatch-roofed huts that were arranged in no apparent order, were clumps of banana and bamboo trees. The entire village was shaded by large trees under which were clearings. The village appeared like an oasis in a green, tropical desert. It was narrow, but long, and the platoon was entering from the east side, moving west along the length of the village about two hundred fifty meters.

Huts were searched. Metal rods, used as probes, were stuck into anything suspicious enough to warrant probing. All eyes were alert for tripwires, VC in the trees, or any other possible encounter that could bring an untimely demise to the men of the First Platoon.

There were no people in the village, but it was evident that humans still lived there. Max came upon a hut. It was a place of Buddhist worship, containing a small statute of Buddha about three feet high. Buddha, who supposedly lived around 500 B.C., was regarded by his followers as a teacher who possessed perfect enlightenment and wisdom. Right living, he taught, would lead one to a hereafter, where the soul existed without a body and was free of all earthly desires and pain. There were writings in Vietnamese on papers attached to the frond walls of the primitive temple. Max left things undisturbed and continued the sweep of the village, wondering whose God was teaching the "right" living.

"Over here, Lieutenant!"

Cpl. Tanner had come upon a 250 pound bomb partially embedded in the ground. Most likely, a U.S. plane had dropped it on the village some time ago, but it didn't detonate. In the rice paddies around the village, huge craters, now filled with water, were testament to the ones that had. Max wondered if the bomb's close proximity to the village temple was a protective omen from Buddha himself. Nevertheless, through the fractured casing of the bomb, the VC had already removed more than enough high explosive to make many booby traps. The bomb would have to be blown in place.

"Corporal Shane, have everyone hold up," Max ordered.

Sergeant Gorman approached. "What's up, Lieutenant?" About the same instant he spoke, he saw the bomb.

"Who is carrying the C-4, Sarge?" Max asked.

"Corporal Tanner. Do you have any C-4?" Gorman called.

"Parker's got some, Sarge" then shouted. "Parker, bring the C-4 to Sgt Gorman."

Max had been trained in land mine warfare and the handling of explosives. He went to work rigging a piece of C-4 explosive and a blasting cap to the side of the bomb.

"Sergeant Gorman, get the men in the trenches," Max ordered. The VC had already dug trenches around the village for their own protection from incoming artillery and air bombings.

"Fire in the hole!" Max yelled from his position in a trench as a warning to his men to keep their heads down.

It was more of an explosion than anticipated. Dirt and debris rained down in a quantity that had he known earlier, would have altered his choice of position. When all settled, Max looked up. To his amazement, there was now a huge crater where once the bomb lay. A new clearing had been made were once banana trees flourished.

"Holy shit," he exclaimed aloud as he saw the temple was gone. The blast had completely disintegrated Buddha's home in Chan Son. "Let's move out!" he ordered and the sweep continued.

At the far end of the village, still with no sign of "Victor Charlie," the sweep ended. If anyone had been in the village, they were driven out the west end and into the mountains, and obviously had chosen to avoid contact with the Americans. "Corporal Shane, advise Kilo Six we have completed the sweep and are at Checkpoint Bravo," Max said.

The patrol now moved south across the paddies until it reached the dirt road. Staggered and spread out, the platoon moved along the edges of the road, walking southeasterly in the direction back towards Thuong Duc.

* * * * * *

It was late afternoon, around 1800 hours, when Max dropped his pack. He was debriefed by the captain who appeared disappointed by the patrol's lack of contact with the enemy.

While eating his evening c-rations, the entree consisting of beans and franks, the sun was sinking behind the mountains to the west. The tall, lanky Marine who had expunged the snake hours earlier, approached and knelt down beside Max.

"I'm glad you let me shoot that snake, Lieutenant," he said.

"I'm glad you didn't miss," Max replied. The Marine smiled. He appeared to be nineteen or twenty years old. "What's your name, Marine?"

"Littlefoot, Sir. Private First Class Littlefoot."

"Do you have a first name PFC Littlefoot?" Max asked.

"No, Sir. I'm a full-blooded American Indian, Navajo tribe. Littlefoot is my full name."

"How long you been in country, Littlefoot?"

"About eight months, Sir, except I was medevaced to Japan last February. Spent three weeks in the hospital there."

"What happened?" Max asked.

"The First Marines were operating up north, near the DMZ. Someone tripped a wire across the trail. Two were killed. Seven wounded in all. I guess I was one of the lucky ones. Took some shrapnel in the back of my neck."

"I'm glad to have you, Littlefoot."

"Glad to have you here, too, Lieutenant. The men liked the way you ran the patrol today."

"Thanks for letting me know that."

Littlefoot nodded, stood up and walked away. Max felt good about his first day with First Platoon.

With barely any daylight left, the third platoon of Kilo Company entered the compound. The men looked physically spent. They had gone out on a three-day patrol, patrolling by day and ambushing by night, leaving little time for sleep. First Lieutenant Mike Cullen was the platoon commander. Max had not had the opportunity to meet him yet, but thought this might not be the best of times to do so.

"Sergeant Gorman," Max called, "set up security in our sector for the night, and I want both M-60's on the line, one at each end. I'm going over to Second Platoon to see Lieutenant Larsen."

"Roger, Lieutenant."

Bob Larsen saw Max approach. "How'd the patrol go today?" he asked.

"Not bad, but if you ever blow a 250 pounder in place, give yourself a wider berth than I did. I almost buried my platoon alive."

Bob laughed and slapped Max on the shoulder. "Have you met Lieutenant Cullen yet?"

"No, thought I'd give him some time to settle in first."

"I suppose I got the day patrol tomorrow and you do the three day deal," Bob said. "Third platoon gets the day off to protect the skipper."

"That seems to be the routine around here," Max stated. "One day patrol, three day patrol, then a day on the hill."

"You know we should be running company-size patrols out of here don't you?" Bob asked.

"Yeah, Sgt. Gorman told me."

"Seems our skipper spent the first seven months of his tour back at Division in a nice cozy staff job," Bob said. "He's a senior captain; been selected for major but needed to get his butt in the bush first. He's got a wife and two kids back home. Seems he's not taking any chances."

"Cullen seems to be doing nothing but having a smoke," Max said. "Let's go introduce ourselves and get some new scoop."

The two men strolled over to meet the Lieutenant in charge of Third Platoon.

"Hi, I'm Max Elliot and this is Bob Larsen. Just arrived today."

"Welcome to paradise gents," Cullen said.

"How'd your patrol go?" Bob asked.

"Not bad, got one VC."

Bob nodded. "Confirmed?"

"You can go confirm him yourself if you want to. We hauled his dead ass back. He's on the other side of the shitter.

"Why'd you bring him back here?"

Mike shrugged. "Captain's orders. Seems the CIA, under the guise of Air America, likes to check out the bodies sometimes".

"Say Mike," Max started out, "you got any words of wisdom for us green guys?"

"Yeah, don't get your ass killed, especially for that asshole, Newbury."

"Do you know the troops got a price on his head?" Max asked.

"Good! I hope they nail him! I've had company commanders before, and they were all hot shit—really good leaders—they looked out for their men. This prick is looking out for his own ass, period."

"Well, we better be getting back to our platoons," Max said. "Thanks for the info."

Sergeant Ualena met Max as he approached. "The skipper is looking for you, Lieutenant."

"Thanks, Sarge, I'm on my way."

Max walked to the entrance of his commander's bunker, and after making himself known, entered.

"Skipper, I understand you wanted to see me," he said.

"You're going on a three day patrol tomorrow," the captain said with his pointer in hand. "Your mission is to secure hill 163 here at coordinates 565182. Recon says there are at least seven VC on the hill now. As you can see, the hill overlooks the road. A small convoy is coming here tomorrow. They're bringing some 155 self-propelled guns with them to set up here on this hill. I want *you* on 163 when that convoy passes, not Victor Charlie. Understand, Lieutenant?" he asked with that familiar distain.

"Yes, Sir, but how long do I stay on the hill?"

"Tomorrow and tomorrow night. Just before dawn on the second day I want you off the hill heading north and then west." Using his pointer, the captain circled six grid squares of mountainous jungle terrain on the map. "I want you to patrol this area by day and ambush at night."

"Anything else, Sir?" Max questioned.

"Yes, Lieutenant, there is. I want you off this hill by 0400 so you can cross the paddies before first light. I suggest you take 163 at dawn."

"But isn't it unwise to move in the dark, Skipper?"

The captain glared at Max. "Just *do* it, Lieutenant," he said, "and I don't want to see you back here before the three days are up. That will be all."

* * * * * *

On his way back to his platoon, Max swung the beam of his flashlight behind the latrine and looked for the body the Third Platoon brought in. He hadn't seen a dead Viet Cong yet. In fact, he wasn't sure if he had even seen a *live* one, unless one of the Vietnamese civilians he had seen was a VC, which of course was possible.

He was startled by the body at first. The corpse was laying face up, eyes open. Flies covered most of the face. Dried blood covered much of the chest and legs. The body was clothed in a black shirt and green trousers, the latter quite similar to the jungle utilities the Americans wore. A sneaker was still on the left foot. The right foot was bare. Not even a sock covered the hole where the M-16 had penetrated. The heel had been blown away, leaving strips of flesh dangling over the cavity. He estimated the deceased's age to be early twenties, if that old. He had also been a small man, perhaps no more than five feet four inches tall.

Max did not sleep well that night. Resting on his air mattress under the stars, he thought about many things; the patrol he would lead in a few short hours, his parents, brothers and sister, and Sally.

He thought about Sally that night. He hadn't received any mail since he'd arrived in country and was eager to hear from home.

Before leaving the U.S., he'd made several trips from Quantico to West Virginia during the year, and Sally had flown in one weekend. They stayed together in a motel near the base. He thought about his final farewell...and their last embrace. Thirteen months seemed like a long time. He wondered if Sally would there for him when he returned. He wasn't sure.

* * * * * *

Sergeant Gorman had the platoon saddled up and ready to move at 0345. There were plenty of stars out, but no moon. Too risky to use their flashlights, they had to do the best they could moving across the paddies in the dark. It was tricky, but except for the men occasionally tripping and the subsequent muffled sound of the four-letter "f" word, at 0520 the platoon reached an area due south of hill 163. The night sky was still black, with no signs of light in the east.

Max unfolded his poncho and spread it on the ground. He told Cpl. Shane to stay close as he crawled under the poncho with his red-lensed light and map. He heard one of the men chuckle. Another said, "What the fuck is he doing?" He ignored their comments.

"Shane, get ready to call in a fire mission," Max said.

"Ready when you are, Lieutenant," the radioman replied. "What are we doing?"

"We're going to make those arty guys at Thuong Duc work for a living. Let's see how good they are," Max said. "We're going to blow the top off hill 163."

"All right!" said Shane.

Sergeant Gorman was nearby and interjected, "Good move, Lieutenant. Beats that John Wayne shit."

"Yeah, but we're still going up," Max said. "We're just gonna give Charlie a little wakeup call first."

After a couple of adjustments, the artillery seemed right on target. It was hard to tell in the dark, but based on his compass azimuth, he was sure the top of 163 had been rearranged.

Shortly thereafter, the eastern sky turned from black to gray and then to a brownish yellow, glowing more brightly by the minute as the top of the sun appeared through the ominous mist ensnared in the paddies around the platoon.

When the light was adequate, the third squad on Max's order, set in at the base of 163 to provide a cover of fire. Moving with the first and second squads, Max directed the men up a draw on the west side of the hill until they were on its flank. On line, he gave the signal to assault the hill.

It was just like he had done a hundred times before in training back in Quantico, only now it was for real. There were rocks and scrub to contend with, but no large trees. Visibility was good, but good also for the VC if they were waiting for them. No shots were fired. The platoon reached the top of the hill with no resistance. Max ordered the third squad up.

"Got one, Lieutenant," called out Corporal Barfield, second squad leader. "I guess they didn't have time to take him with them."

The hill was littered with gear that had been blown to bits; canteens, packs, an SKS rifle with part of its wooden stock gone, and various other debris. The Viet Cong's body had been shredded by shrapnel. His face bore that ghostly look of death Max had seen on the face of the corpse the third platoon had brought in the night prior. Eyes wide open, as was the mouth, with part of the lower jaw blown away exposing the upper teeth and cartilage.

The abdomen was turned inside out, a sickening sight, with bloody intestines strewn from its point of origin to a point several feet away. Max searched the body for any papers that might be of some intelligence value, being careful not to get blood on his hands.

The irony of not wanting to get blood on his hands crossed his mind as he realized the death of another human being was at his direction, and he would always have blood on his hands. He took a shaky breath, keeping his head low, then let it out slowly. He would always be responsible for that loss of life and others to come.

He ordered a spot report sent back to the captain confirming one VC KIA.

As the sun rose in the sky, the heat on the treeless hill became intense. Kilo One set up perimeter security and waited for the convoy. Except for those on watch, most of the men relaxed, some trying to catch a little sleep.

The dry dust on the hilltop mixed with the sweat on Max's body. He hadn't had a bath or shower in three days. His men had not bathed in at least two weeks. His new boots were now covered with dried mud, and he hadn't shaved in several days. Max Elliot was beginning to feel "salty," and he liked that.

The hours passed and the sun showed no mercy. Having lived in Florida as a young child, he was somewhat accustomed to temperatures in the mid-nineties, along with high humidity. Here, however, without any shade for relief, it must have been about 110 degrees, along with the thick humidity. He reached for one of the four canteens he carried on his web belt. He unscrewed the top and swallowed a large gulp, gagging on the warm, iodine-purified brown river water.

At around 1330, the platoon could see the dust cloud along the road to the east as the convoy slowly made its way west. As it neared, they observed two Marines walking ahead of a tank sweeping the road for mines as they moved. Just then, they saw a puff of smoke from the front end of the tank, followed by the sound of the explosion as it echoed in the valley.

Looking through his binoculars Max could see a half dozen or so Marines at the sight rush to aid the tank driver whose now bloody head protruded from his position forward of the turret. The minesweepers had missed one, and the force of the explosion had broken off part of the track that swung up and over, wounding the driver. A medevac was called in.

The convoy was halted and could go nowhere until the tank was repaired, as it blocked the narrow road. If the other tank in the rear of the convoy, or one of the self propelled 155 guns should try to pass by going into the rice paddy, it would surely sink in the mud up to its turret, to remain there for eternity. Once mired in the mud, not even a tank retriever could overcome the suction to free such a heavy vehicle. Blown in place and burned internally with a white phosphorous grenade, these monuments to war remain scattered about in South Vietnam.

Tended by a corpsman, the wounded Marine was airlifted out in about thirty-five minutes. It took until almost 1600 to repair the tank and get the convoy rolling once again. They still had enough daylight left to reach Thuong Duc in time. Meanwhile, the First Platoon remained in position on the hill.

Shortly after sunset, Max ordered each squad to send out a listening post a short distance in front of the platoon's perimeter. Each LP set a claymore in front of its position. It was a long tense night, not knowing if "Charlie" might counterattack and get his revenge against the Americans.

Max ordered a fifty percent alert, so each man could sleep every other hour when the Marine next to him took the watch. Everyone wore their helmets and flak jackets and was in position to fight should they have to.

Even those that enjoyed their hour's sleep were ready and in position.

Relief from the torturous sun at nightfall was replaced by a plague of mosquitoes and other insects, both flying and crawling. The men carried small plastic bottles of GI issued insect repellant they called "bugfuck," a euphemism typical of America's finest. Max spread the greasy, smelly liquid on his neck, face and hands, the only exposed parts of his body. It burned slightly, and mixed with the sweat and dirt, he felt rank.

The mosquitoes didn't go away—instead, they swarmed by the thousands within inches of his ears. Occasionally, one brave bug would penetrate the perimeter of insecticide and commence sucking his blood, only to be slapped to its death. Stinging ants, apparently escaping the intense heat of the day by living underground, made their debut at night, biting viciously. Max had never had a longer night. He shared the watch with Cpl. Shane and Sgt. Gorman. When manning the radio, he occasionally called each squad to make certain people were awake and alert.

The squad leaders in turn made certain their LP's, the platoon's first line of defense, were awake. The time moved at an incredibly slow pace. Minutes seemed like hours. Hours seemed like forever.

Finally, dawn broke. The LP's were brought in and the smell of heat tabs filled the air as men tried to heat coffee in their canteen cups over the little blue flames. The corpse had been dumped on the far side of the hill, but was decaying quickly in the heat. The body odor of the members of First Platoon, along with the fetid "bugfuck," and human excretions disposed of quietly in the night, all combined to tax the olfactory organs heavily. Max did not feel much like eating anything, but graciously accepted a swig of not-too-hot black coffee offered by Cpl. Shane.

It was time to move out. Cpl. Tanner's squad took the lead position. PFC Ingersoll, the shortest man in the platoon volunteered to walk point.

At 6'3", Lance Corporal Pomeroy was an inch taller than Max. Blond, with piercing blue eyes, Pomeroy aspired to become a State Trooper in his home state of Nevada after his enlistment.

Moving north, the foothills quickly turned to mountainous jungle. While shaded from the unforgiving sun by the double and triple canopy provided by the trees, it was unbearably hot. Looking ahead at the men in front of him, Max saw steam coming off their bodies.

As the sweat poured down his face, his eyes burned. Soon the old animal trail they followed came to an end at a rocky streambed. Ingersoll held up to consult with Cpl. Tanner. Tanner, in turn, summoned, "Lieutenant up."

Signaling the platoon to get down on one knee, Max quietly moved forward to Tanner's position. There were no other obvious trails and the jungle was so thick that the only way through it would be to cut through with machetes, a method not only slow and tiresome, but noisy as well. Max ordered Tanner to move up the stream bed.

The patrol continued. The water coming out of the higher mountains ran clear and cool. The men dumped what was left of the river water from their canteens and filled up on the water from the stream. Max removed his steel helmet and with a single scoop, poured a helmet full of water over his head. It felt good and offered temporary relief. The mountainside grew increasingly steep. The men began to trip and fall over the large boulders as the water cascaded downward toward the valley floor.

After a while, Ingersoll again stopped. Again, Max moved forward to consult with Cpl. Tanner and PFC Ingersoll. Ingersoll had come upon another trail, this one leading off in a westerly direction from the stream. The jungle was eerie. The usual sounds of birds and other animals were silent.

Max's sixth sense told him that "Charlie" was near, perhaps watching First Platoon's movement that very moment. All the men felt it and no one made a sound. In a low whisper, Max told Ingersoll to take the trail, knowing the VC couldn't move through trees anymore than they could. Their mission after-all, the sole purpose of day two of the three-day patrol, was to seek out and destroy the enemy.

Perhaps forty yards up the trail the silence was broken by the crackling of automatic weapons fire. Instinctively, everyone got down seeking some form of cover. Max felt his stomach lurch.

This was his moment of truth—his first real firefight. He had heard of one 2nd Lieutenant who cowardly curled into a fetal position during a similar moment in his career. It happened fast. Max heard Ingersoll's scream.

"I'm hit!"

The adrenalin kicked in within milliseconds. "First Squad up!" Max commanded loudly. As they did so, the squad immediately put out a large volume of automatic gunfire in the direction of the enemy.

As Max moved forward, Tanner and Pomeroy dragged Ingersoll back to a point out of harm's way. Doc Shepherd went to work on him. Suddenly, Max heard the incoming rounds from the enemy's automatic weapons crackling around him. Cpl. Shane, only a few yards away, dove behind a large rock.

"Get down, Lieutenant!" he screamed.

Almost concurrently, Max hit the earth behind another small boulder. The fusillade seemed directed right at him as it chipped away at the stone protection in front of him, which was no more than two feet high.

First Squad had taken cover and was returning fire. The enemy was no more than fifteen or twenty yards away, yet they were invisible in the thick jungle.

Cpl. Shane was on the radio talking to Captain Newbury. "The captain wants to know how close they are, Lieutenant."

"Ask him if he wants to talk to them!" Max yelled back above the clamor of the weapons. And then he saw the chi-com grenade tumble through the air. It landed within arm's reach on his left side.

Shit! What the hell? Reach out, grab it and throw it away? Yeah—end up with one arm. *Shit!*

Instead, he put his head down, held onto his helmet and prayed. Holding his breath and clinching his teeth, he heard himself make a grimacing sound in anticipation.

For a long moment there was silence. He opened his eyes and let out his breath. A dud. Those few seconds of divine decision on Max's mortality were undoubtedly the longest few seconds of his twenty-two-year existence.

"I thought we were goners, Lieutenant!" Shane hollered.

"That son-of-a-bitch tried to *kill* me!" Max screeched back to Shane. With gunfire all around, bullets coming in and going out, he determined he was not going to give "Charlie" another opportunity to kill him.

He rolled onto his right side and removed one of the four grenades he carried in his pouch. He pulled the pin, careful not to let the spoon fly, and then hurled the grenade with a force equivalent to that of a major league baseball pitcher. The ensuing explosion broke the ambush.

First Squad moved forward about ten meters firing automatic bursts into the dense jungle ahead. They never saw any of the VC they were shooting at until they came upon two bodies on the ground at the point they ceased the pursuit.

In the shooting frenzy, several of the squad members had emptied their magazines into the already dead enemy. One of the guerrillas had a hole in the right side of his head the size of a nickel, but on the left side the skull was gone almost entirely. The grey matter indicative of the superior intelligence of homo sapiens lay alongside the cavity.

"Sgt. Gorman!" Max called out.

"Over here, Lieutenant!"

"Where the hell you been?" Max questioned as Gorman ran up.

"Back with the Third Squad, watching our rear," Gorman asserted.

"The firefight was up here, not back there! Never mind, any other casualties?" Max asked.

"Not that I know of. He moaned when he was moved, but Ingersoll was still alive, even if he was critically wounded."

Pomeroy insisted on carrying one end of the litter that contained his best friend. Just before they started out, Ingersoll closed his eyes and his head rolled to the side. Frantic, Pomeroy yelled out his fallen comrade's name.

"Ingersoll! Ingersoll!"

And as if called back from the dead, Ingersoll slowly opened his eyes and looked at Pomeroy. Pomeroy responded, "You do that again and I'll kill you!"

After a nervous chuckle rippled through the squad, they moved out towards the valley floor to meet the medevac chopper that Max radioed for as the rest of the platoon headed in a southwesterly direction in pursuit of the VC. Ingersoll was still alive when he was put on the chopper.

The First Squad remained on the landing zone at Max's direction. Not long into the pursuit, the platoon happened upon a small tunnel complex. Max held up his .45 and asked for a volunteer. With Ingersoll gone he needed another "tunnel rat" to check out the tunnel.

There were two openings in the hillside. PFC Mendez, also not a particularly large man, accepted the pistol and entered the tunnel.

Max listened for gunfire, wondering what he could do to help Mendez if he ran into trouble but was rewarded long minutes later when the PFC returned to report.

"It went in about thirty feet and curved around, coming back out the other opening that was about another thirty feet from where I went in. "Some clothes and some rice balls, that's all I found."

Max radioed the First Squad and arranged to link up with them at a point midway between the two units. They did as planned, all the time radioing their position back to the company commander. A situation report had been sent advising of the ambush, the two VC KIA's, and the one Marine wounded in action.

Max wasn't toting their corpses back to base. The VC bodies were left to decompose like they'd leave an apple core to rot.

Max thought about the bodies. *They must have families...will they ever learn the fate of their loved ones?* Should he feel badly over the death of enemy soldiers?

The first platoon continued on patrol the remainder of the day. Max picked his ambush site for the night, moved through it and immediately after dark went back to it and set in.

It was another long, insect infested night. The men were exhausted. The night seemed to pass more quickly than the previous night, probably because sleep from exhaustion came more easily when it was time to sleep. That one-hour allotted every other hour went by in a flash, so the nine hours or so of darkness appeared to pass in half the time.

Just before dawn, they vacated the ambush site and the platoon continued on its patrol. They would spend much of the third day looking for the enemy, but by the afternoon they'd start heading back to Thuong Duc, a place that falsely offered security. But, it was better than being in the jungle. The hours passed with no enemy contact. By late afternoon, the platoon headed south out of the mountains on a trail leading to the valley floor. From there it was just two clicks to Thuong Duc.

With the sun low on the horizon, it was starting to cool just slightly and after humping up and down the mountains for two days it was uplifting to be going downhill on the last leg of the patrol.

Max sensed the renewed vitality in his men. He heard one man say to another he hoped there would be mail when they got back. Max agreed. Just then a call came over the radio.

"Kilo One, Kilo One, this is Kilo."

Shane acknowledged, "Kilo, this is Kilo One, go."

"Kilo Six wants to speak with One Actual."

"Roger, wait one," Shane replied.

"Lieutenant, Kilo Six wants you on the horn."

Max took the handset from Cpl. Shane. "Kilo Actual, Kilo One here, go."

"Kilo One, I want you to alter your route to check out the following coordinates: from rose, north two point two, west point seven. Do you copy?"

"Roger Kilo, I've got a solid copy, but my position now puts me closer to your pos, and we're on our way in."

The company commander's reply was not what Max wanted to hear. "Negative One, I want that area checked! \ Kilo out." The radio went silent.

Max ground his teeth and pulled out the map. He looked for the grid coordinates the captain wanted them to patrol. Rather than being given the actual coordinates, a code was used so as not to give the enemy their position should they be monitoring their radio frequency.

"Shit!" Max muttered. "He wants us to move through the exact spot we were ambushed in, only this time coming in from the trail to the west."

"What are we gonna do, Lieutenant?" asked Sgt. Gorman.

"We got our orders. Turn the platoon around and let's start moving."

There was grumbling among the men and Max couldn't blame them. He couldn't even swallow the bitterness *he* felt. The men of First Platoon, most of who were nineteen or twenty years old, were Marines, and infantry Marines at that. And the captain had no respect.

Max gave them a few minutes to check ammunition and adjust packs. His mind was raging. It was the young infantrymen like *his* men who fought the war. They did the killing and they did the dying. The rear echelon staff people couldn't even imagine what the life of the "grunt" was like.

He thought back to his college days, to conversations with frat brothers and even Sally. These men gave up being home in comfy suburbia. They gave up hot showers, beds, movies and hot meals. Now on the third day of a three-day patrol, exhausted, hungry, filthy and discouraged, they were being asked to once again test the limits of their physical and psychological endurance. *Fuck you. Sir.*

The platoon moved uphill. Each step an effort. Each man suffering in silence as one foot forcibly moved in front of the other. Sweat beaded on their heads, dripping down from beneath their steel helmets only to sting their eyes with its solution of salt and dirt.

Near the crest of the ridge, the trail turned more easterly. The men moved quietly. The occasional sound of a rifle sling or other gear jingling were the only sounds over the heavy breathing of the men. The jungle thickened once again and the tall treetops formed their canopy under which bright daylight rapidly gave way to a ghostly shade of gray. With the sun already low on the horizon, darkness in the jungle was encroaching all too soon.

Corporal Garrison stopped and called for his Lieutenant. Max crouched low and jogged forward to Garrison's position, getting down on one knee as he arrived.

It was dead quiet. Not a bird, not a breeze moving a tree limb, not a sound. It was as if all living things, even the vegetation, held its breath in anticipation of the pending chaotic moment when the stillness would erupt into violence.

The jungle knew what was about to happen. Max felt it, too. He thought he could hear his own heartbeat and wondered if Corporal Garrison could hear it.

"Are we going down there, Lieutenant?" Garrison asked.

Max looked ahead at the trail as it curved ominously to the east and then downwards into darkness, like a tunnel into hell, the gateway to Hades. His throat felt dry and scratchy. He had his orders and he was trained not to disobey orders, yet he knew that Captain Newbury himself was disobeying orders from Battalion by not conducting company-size patrols.

Was that reason enough for him to disobey an order? Max knew, as well as every one of the men of the first platoon, that to enter that tunnel of darkness was to tempt the devil himself; to say here I am, now let's see who wins.

Max was scared. They were *all* scared. But it was not fear that prevented him from giving the order to move on. It was the insanity of the plan.

Traversing jungle trails in darkness was just plain stupid. Tripwires could not be seen. The enemy, though probably well hidden, could not be seen except for the muzzle flashes after the fact—after springing his ambush and after the realm of darkness was made a permanent entity for some, or all.

Max looked at Cpl. Garrison's radio operator and whispered, "Get me squad leaders and Sgt. Gorman up."

In a moment Sgt. Gorman, Cpl. Tanner and Cpl. Barfield were down on one knee joining Max and Cpl. Garrison. They too looked at the forbidding trail that lay ahead and below. Their eyes were wide in anticipation of Max's next move.

"Our orders are to move through this area ahead, move around the mountain, come out on the east side. From there, we can find our way south to the valley floor."

"Lieutenant, if we go in there, we're going to run into deep shit," said Cpl. Barfield.

Cpl. Tanner was next to speak. "You know Charlie's in there just waiting for us, right Lieutenant?"

These were not green troops. All three of the squad leaders had seen a lot of action. They were seasoned combat Marines and Max did not take their comments as cowardice. These men had seen the face of death and didn't want to tempt it unnecessarily. Still, orders were orders.

"I'd be disobeying a direct order from the skipper if we don't proceed," Max stated.

"Ain't nobody gonna tell, Lieutenant," said Cpl. Tanner.

The others nodded in agreement. Sgt. Gorman said, "It would be suicide to move through there in the dark, Lieutenant."

"It's my ass if the skipper finds out we didn't go."

"Don't worry about that, he'll never find out," Sgt. Gorman added. "We'll suffer heavy casualties if we go in there and you know it."

Max sighed, but he knew he was right. "Okay then, let's make the tail the point and the point the tail and get the fuck out of here!" He knew it was not wise to cover the same trail going back, but in this terrain there was little choice.

Besides, Max wanted out of there and quick. He wanted the platoon out of the mountains while there was still some daylight left. The pace quickened as once again the First Platoon moved westward and downward along the old French trail that descended from the higher elevations. Max was certain everyone felt relieved at his decision, as did he, although he was troubled at having disobeyed an order.

Hell with it. He was confident that lives were saved and for that, he felt better.

CHAPTER 6

Australia

When the weather cooled in March, attention turned to breaking some of the two-year old stock horses. Amber enjoyed watching and was especially entertained when a jackaroo got thrown. Usually no one got hurt, other than the pride of a young rider with a mouth full of dirt.

But on this day Amber wasn't amused. The nausea was recurring with greater frequency. She was pregnant, but she told no one, not even Gordon. Her parents would be devastated and John would probably kill Gordon when he found out. She was desperate for a solution. She thought about an abortion, but for someone who loved all life and went to extraordinary measures to save a sick or injured calf, foal or kitten, abortion was out of the question.

Her only solution would be to tell Gordon first. It took her days to get up the courage. Then she told him.

"How do I know the baby is mine?" he said.

The slap across his face came so quickly he didn't have a chance to react. His cheek was red with the imprint of her hand and his hat knocked awry on his head.

"How dare you, you bastard!"

"Take it easy. I'm sorry," he said. "You just caught me by surprise."

"What am I going to do?" she whispered as the tears swelled in her gorgeous green eyes.

Gordon placed his hands on each side of her face and with his thumbs wiped the tears. He stroked her hair gently before embracing her. "We'll work something out, don't worry."

"Don't worry! I'm pregnant and you say don't worry! Easy for you to say!"

"I'll take care of you, promise."

Delia McEwen was a kind and understanding woman who cherished her family above all else. Amber finally told her mother.

Shocked, hurt, in disbelief; none the less she was compassionate with her daughter whom she held in her arms as they sat on the bed and rocked back and forth, the younger McEwen consumed with emotion and tears.

George McEwen was the most adversely affected. Usually a strong man emotionally, he withdrew into his own privacy, unable initially to face his daughter in whom he was now immeasurably disappointed.

John was right, he thought in the silence of his study. *We should have thrown that son-of-a-bitch off the Sunrise.*

John was not so understanding when his father told him, and the fire in his eyes glowed with savage vividness. Gordon was by the paddock talking with Cory Gardner and Billy Sidders, two other jackaroos on the ranch, when John attacked.

Gordon barely saw him coming when John's fist busted his lip wide open. "I'll kill you for this, you bloody bastard!" John shouted as he came in for the next volley.

"Hold on man!" Gordon cried out as he blocked John's next blow. John struck him hard in the ribs. Gordon grimaced as he bent forward. The uppercut lifted him upwards and back as his knees quivered and he almost fell.

But Gordon Hamilton had seen his fair share of knuckle-cutting encounters and he had taken enough abuse for one day. He blocked John's right hook and landed a solid blow to John's jaw.

Billy and Cory stepped back as the two men had at it, not attempting to stop the fight. John shook his head from the shock of the punch and went at Gordon again. Blood spewed from Gordon's mouth while the cut above John's eye bled.

"Stop it! Stop it!" Amber screamed as she ran to them from the house. "Stop it now!"

Just then the elder McEwen jumped between the two combatants. "Hold on boys," he spoke with authority. Panting, the two men stood posed for further battle, but refrained. "Let's go up to the house and talk this matter out."

Amber and her mother, who was now also by the paddock, embraced each other as they followed the three men to the house.

* * * * * *

"Delia, get a couple of washrags for these boys so they don't bleed all over the floor".

The elder McEwen spoke first as the three sat in a room isolated from the women. "What do you have in mind Mr. Hamilton, so far as the welfare of my daughter is concerned"?

"Well Sir, I haven't quite sorted that out just yet."

"Do you love her?" the elder McEwen asked.

Gordon scratched his chin and hesitated in answering as he searched for the right words.

John exploded. "See, Father? He can't answer that honestly. He took advantage of Amber, that's all. He used her."

"That's not entirely true, John. I *do* care about her," Gordon said.

"You care about her, you say," John said with consternation. "Father, I say we run the bloody bastard clear out of the territory and back to Queensland where he came from."

"Perhaps we will son, but first let's give Mr. Hamilton here a little time to advise us of his intentions. Gordon, I want you to think real hard tonight about what you plan on doing about this situation and come see me tomorrow. You got that?"

"Yes Sir, sure do."

"Good, now both you boys get cleaned up and tend to those cuts before you bleed to death."

As John and Gordon left the room, Delia and her daughter entered. George sat in his large red leather chair bearing a disheartening frown. "Amber, how could you?" he lamented.

"I am so sorry, Father. I know I have disappointed you greatly. But Gordon loves me," she said woefully.

"Do you love *him*, darling?" asked Delia.

"Yes, I love him Mother. Gordon will marry me and we'll have this baby. We'll be a family together."

* * * * * *

Later that evening Amber approached Gordon for a heart-to-heart. To her disappointment, Gordon was not so committal about love *or* marriage.

"Look, you know how much I care for you, but marriage? I'm not ready for that just yet," he said.

"And just when will you be ready? When our baby is all grown up? Just tell me you love me, Gordon."

"Sure I love you, but I think it would be wise if I left Sunrise for awhile...to sort things out."

"Then I'm going with you!"

"Nah, I think it would be best if you stay here with your family."

"Gordon Hamilton, I am going to have your baby, and where you go, I and this baby are going as well!"

"But your parents would never approve," he said.

"They don't have to approve. I am going with you."

Gordon could not have been more correct. "Mr. McEwen," he said during his encounter the following day, "Amber and I have agreed it would be best if we left the Sunrise."

"Left! Just where do you think you're taking my daughter?"

"I thought we would head up to Moree. I have a friend who runs a large spread up there. We can settle in there for a spell."

"Young man, you can go settle in there or anywhere else you damn well please, but my daughter is not going anywhere! Do you understand?"

"I think you better have a talk with your daughter then, Mr. McEwen," Gordon said as he turned and left just as Amber, who was waiting in the hallway walked in.

"Amber, I forbid you to go anywhere with that man."

"Father, I love him and he loves me. I am going with him!"

Delia interjected. "Amber darling, he's no good for you. What life is there for you following a jackaroo around the continent?"

"I'm sorry Mother. I must leave with Gordon." With that Amber stormed from the room.

"Let her go, Delia," George said. "She'll be back before the wet season."

"I'm worried about her George. She's carrying a baby. She will need me...she will need *us*".

"Like I said, she'll be back sooner than you know. That Hamilton bloke will show his true colors and she'll be back, you'll see."

John made one final effort to convince his sister not to run off with the likes of Hamilton, but to no avail. "If he mistreats you in anyway, I'll shear his hide, so help me I will!"

"I love you John. You're as good a brother as any girl could ask for, but I'll be just fine. Gordon loves me and will take good care of me, or *us*, I should say." She clasped her hands over her abdomen. "Take care of Tuffy for me, will you?"

"Sure, just take care of yourself, will you do that for me?"

"I'll be fine."

* * * * *

The dust was still visible in the distance as Hamilton's old truck headed north. Delia watched her daughter leave, then broke down. Crying, she ran to the house.

"This is a big mistake, Father," John asserted.

"I know it is son, but that sister of yours is as headstrong as a rogue dingo. She's going to have to learn."

CHAPTER 7

Thuong Duc, July 1968

The beer was warm and rationed infrequently...maybe one per man about once a week. Buried in the ground overnight, it was usually consumed as breakfast. While not cold, its temperature was reduced from hot to that of the ambient earth where it had spent the nocturnal hours.

C-rations and hot coffee...a few hours of sleep under a makeshift shelter out of the direct rays of the broiling sun...time to write a letter home or to read again for the umpteenth time that last letter received a week ago... these were the simple pleasures of the infantryman.

As Sgt. Gorman read aloud from the envelopes he held before him, each man hoped he would hear his name called so he could step forward and receive his mail.

Max received several letters, one postmarked West Virginia. He read that one first.

Sally had spent the summer at the university taking a couple of courses to ease her fall class workload. Since there was not much to do back in her home town of Beckley over the summer, taking courses in Morgantown was a good excuse to be on campus. While she inquired about how Max was holding up, the letter pertained to the things she was doing at school. A summer concert by the "Four Seasons," a tough exam, a wild party at Crystal Lake and a summer roommate's personal problems.

For Max, all those things seemed incredibly far away in terms of time and distance. Even though he was only out of college fourteen months, the memories of college life seemed much more distant.

What was going on at the college and the things Sally was doing seemed trite and insignificant. Hell, he was killing people. He couldn't shower or shave most of the time. Men his age and older depended on him to go home alive.

Shit, in Nam, everyday was a struggle to survive and the reality was that death could be imminent. Sally was completely clueless. *But how could she know?*

How could anyone not living the nightmare know what it was *really* like to be a part of it? *Was this not to be the ultimate adventure?* Was there really no glory to war after all? It sure as hell wasn't anything like that poster the recruiter had given him.

The resupply chopper brought six of First Platoon's men back from the rear. Lance Corporal Sealy was returning from R & R in Bangkok. Four others had been recovering from various ailments at the Battalion Aid Station.

Lance Corporal McCarthy had a toothache tended to by the dentist. PFC Keaton and PFC Jackson both had malaria. PFC Corbett had a broken ankle. The sixth man was Pvt. Dawson, returning from thirty days of brig time for striking his squad leader.

"Watch Dawson Lieutenant," said Sgt. Gorman. "He's a bad ass."

"How's that?"

"He just doesn't go along with the program. He's a real loner—keeps to himself. None of the men like him or trust him. Punched out Corporal Tanner because Tanner was chewing him out for sleeping on post. He should have been court-martialed for that but was only charged with striking an NCO."

"What about the guy with the cast on his ankle?"

"That's Corbett. He's the only other turd in this outfit. Rumor has it he had one of his buddies deliberately break his ankle by smashing it with a large rock. He figures this way he don't have to go out on patrol."

"What about the man who smashed Corbett's ankle? Anybody questioned him?" Max asked.

"That's just it. He rotated back to the world the next day, so no one really had the opportunity."

"So Dawson's a shit-bird and Corbett's a malingerer. Anyone else I need to know about Sarge?"

"No Sir, the rest of the platoon are first class Marines."

The days rolled into weeks as the war continued. K Company remained at Thuong Duc as part of operation Mameluke Thrust.

The routine continued. It was one day on the hill, one day patrolling the surrounding hamlets in the Vu Gia valley and the dreaded three-day patrol.

Pvt. Dawson kept much to himself during the ensuing weeks. He obeyed orders, but barely. Max transferred him to the third squad under the leadership of Cpl. Garrison. Dawson went on patrols but was always reticent and never willingly offered to carry link ammo for the M-60, a LAAW- a light anti-tank weapon used to take out enemy fortifications or a 60mm mortar round. He became increasingly friendly with, of all people, PFC Corbett, who was in the second squad. Corbett couldn't go on patrol due to his ankle, but Max kept him busy filling sandbags.

During those weeks, there was no major contact with the VC or NVA. Patrols encountered sniper fire. One man was wounded in Larsen's platoon.

One man in Lt. Cullen's platoon stepped on a booby-trapped rice paddy dike and lost a foot. The small explosive devices referred to as "toe poppers," usually took the foot along with the toes. "Foot poppers" was probably a more appropriate name for them.

The mama-san and papa-san working in the adjacent rice paddy when the explosion and subsequent traumatic amputation of PFC Hemphill's foot took place were taken into custody by Lt. Cullen and sent back to Battalion on a chopper for interrogation. Such persons were classified as "detainees" and not prisoners until such time as they were proven to be VC.

The civilians in the little fishing village of Thuong Duc situated at the foot of the hill the Marines occupied, kept to themselves. They worked nets strung across the river to trap fish swimming downstream and used small homemade boats to harvest their catch.

Children from the village sometimes ventured up the south side of the hill to a point just below the razor sharp concertina wire the Marines had placed around the company's perimeter. Jumping up and down while waving their arms, the children shouted, "GI number one, VC number ten, gimme chop-chop!"

To the Marines, c-rations were nothing more than a distasteful substance, many left over from the Korean War, to fill an abdominal void while concurrently providing nourishment. Well, they were *told* there was nutritional value.

But to the Vietnamese, c-rats were a welcomed gastrointestinal extravaganza. It was policy, however, not to give c-rations to the civilians, as what they *really* wanted were the empty cans to make explosive devices— not so much what was in the cans.

One day as the children again begged for "chop-chop," Corporal Tanner hurled a can of rations across the wire. The children, at least ten of then, scrambled to get the can.

As one kid fell on the can others piled on top, making it look more like they were recovering a fumble in a football game. Tanner followed the throw with another. Again the children lunged for the anticipated can of food until it made a popping sound and a cloud of noxious CS gas filled the surrounding air.

The children dispersed, screaming and gagging. Max reprimanded Cpl. Tanner for his actions. The children, none-the-less, ceased climbing the hill to beg for food. *Is this any way "to win the hearts and minds of the people?*

Of the three-day patrols First Platoon was ordered to go on, only one was to the west. None of the platoons had patrolled to the west before. All the patrols executed by the company, or rather by the platoons of the company, as Captain Newbury had yet to leave the hill, were either to the north, east or south.

Since Kilo Company was the last friendly unit west of Danang, possibly not a single patrol in the entire Division had ever ventured west of Thuong Duc, with the possible exception of recon inserts who were put in to observe and were then extracted by helicopter.

Max's orders were to patrol in a westerly direction approximately twenty five hundred meters to hill 551, then south about twelve hundred meters to a point overlooking a concrete bridge built by the French during their occupancy.

A night ambush had to be set up close to the bridge. Physically, the patrol proved to be the most arduous the platoon had yet encountered. The jungle was incredibly thick with vegetation. Machetes had to be used even on what little trails could be followed. The hills were brutally steep.

As they reached one ridgeline, the next one appeared ahead, with a journey between that meant a descent and then another climb with the descents into the draw proving as unbearable as the climb up the next finger.

The men slipped and fell as the vibram lug soles of their jungle boots broke free of their hold on terra firma. Machine-guns were handed down by rope. The silence intended was sporadically broken by the momentary clamor of military hardware followed by a four-letter word.

Drenched with sweat, exhausted and deeply concerned about the reported large NVA unit in the area, the platoon set up security and rested on the summit of hill 551.

Contour intervals on military maps prepared by the Army Map Service depicted a change in elevation of twenty meters. Hill 551 had an elevation of 551 meters or one thousand eight hundred and seven feet above the valley floor. Not exactly Mt. Kilimanjaro and actually less than one tenth the height of Africa's highest peak, none the less, the Army Map Service, in a footnote in the map legend made a statement about the surrounding area the first platoon had just traversed.

Dense jungle concealed by canopy with undergrowth generally impassable on foot.

"So much for Captain Newbury and his fucking patrol", Max muttered. Too late in the day and too fatigued to continue, Kilo One set in for the night.

Max set the platoon in a 360-degree perimeter defense. LP's were sent out, but not far. A fifty percent alert was maintained throughout the long, quiet night. Everyone kept low, as the rule in any tactical night position was anything walking gets shot.

And once again after a long stressful night, the eastern sky turned gray and finally the outline of the sun appeared over the mountains behind the dismal mist. It was good to see the sun and to be alive for another day. One member of the platoon mimicked the radio announcer on AFVN radio with, "gooooood morning Vietnam!"

After a hasty breakfast of cold c's, First Platoon mounted up and moved south. It was downhill for the next one thousand meters. There were no trails to follow and one misstep could mean death in a deep draw.

Max plotted a compass heading and navigated through the impenetrable jungle literally from tree to tree. PFC Jackson, walking point, swung a machete as he labored forward and downward. The temperature at dawn was already sweltering and oppressive in nature's torrid sauna.

Hour after hour the platoon hacked its way through the mountainous jungle. About mid afternoon, at an elevation of approximately one hundred sixty meters, the vegetation thinned slightly to where PFC Jackson could carry his M-16 instead of the machete. After another steep descent of forty meters, Jackson halted and called back for the lieutenant.

Incredibly, the platoon had happened upon a bunker. Completely overgrown with vines and other vegetation, the octagonal concrete structure protruded from the ground about four feet. Its top and side walls were eight inches thick.

Jackson entered the bunker through its small opening on the east side. Other than its inhabitants of insects, spiders and a snake, the latter curled in a corner of the dirt floor, it appeared no human had visited the structure in many years. Maybe not since the French had built it during their years of attempted colonization.

"What now, Lieutenant?" questioned Sgt. Gorman.

Analyzing the situation, Max knew why the French would build such a mini- fortress in that spot. "Look to the south through that brush, Sarge," Max said.

"Well I'll be damn! There's the bridge down there. That sucker's all concrete too! I was expecting some wooden piece-of-shit bridge."

"The French were here to stay. Everything they built in this country, they built of concrete. This bunker was obviously built to observe and protect the bridge down there."

Corporal Garrison was standing by. "But why would they bust their asses to build a bridge way the hell out here? It don't go nowhere."

"Wrong. Look at my map," Max said. "This dirt road runs along the north side of the river, crosses the bridge, then follows the river west along its south side for another fifteen hundred meters. From that point, the road heads southwesterly through the mountains probably to the Ho Chi Minh trail. This map doesn't go that far, but we're not too far from the Laotian border."

"Are we setting up here, Lieutenant?" Cpl. Garrison asked.

"For now we are. Sgt. Gorman, let's set up a perimeter defense. I want a small work detail to clear the vines and shit off the top of this bunker and cut away some of the growth obstructing our view of the bridge.

"Just before dark, Cpl. Garrison, you and Cpl. Barfield will take your squads down and set up an ambush site in those hedgerows on this side of the river. Corporal Tanner, your squad will stay here with me. We'll set up our CP on the roof of this bunker and watch the bridge through the starlight scope. Let's get to work".

* * * * * *

The two squads headed down the ridgeline for the river. Fighting bone-deep fatigue, Max perched himself on top of the bunker and for most of the night peered through the starlight scope at the bridge below, waiting for an unknown-sized force of unsuspecting enemy to walk into the kill zone of interlocking fields of fire.

The second and third squads furtively waited for the appropriate moment when the blast of their claymores and the fusillade of their machine-guns and M-16s would break the silence of the night; when during such a brief interlude of killing frenzy—the commodity of war—death would come to pass.

Over-fatigued, the eyes played games with his mind. Several times Max thought he saw an army of men marching across the bridge. He pulled his eye away from the scope and shook his head, only to look once again at the green world as seen through the scope, and the army would be no more.

Physically spent, Max could no longer look through the scope and separate reality from imagination. He handed the scope to Sgt. Ualena, put his head on his pack and was immediately asleep. In one hour, Cpl. Shane quietly woke him as directed. Max resumed his observation, but on that night the insurgents remained elusive.

Morning once again...one of the few luxuries looked forward to. The CP and first squad moved down the face of the finger and joined up with the other two squads. Nonchalance was a killer. More than one unit had sat in an ambush only to have every member of that unit fall asleep. One squad from First Marines was found one morning, each man executed by a bullet through his brain. Other than the naked corpses, the VC took everything.

* * * * * *

Late one night in early August, after almost fifty days at Thuong Duc, the enemy attacked the hill. Fortunately, Captain Newbury had kept the entire company on the hill following a recon insert report of an NVA Regiment in the area.

Incoming mortar rounds rocked the earth while the Marines' mortars and artillery returned the favors. The blasts from the 155's were in rapid succession. A sapper, attempting to breach the wire perimeter, was gunned down by machine-gun fire as flares lit the night sky.

Enemy soldiers darted from side to side outside the wire as flares ignited. Tracer rounds from the M-60's sprayed the hillside. The explosive sounds of the 155 guns and the 105 howitzers sending out their ordinance shook the ground like a deafening earthquake.

Captain Newbury, from within his sandbagged bunker, shouted commands over the radio but was barely audible and mostly ignored during the chaos. Max, crouching low, ran through the trenches giving orders with Cpl. Shane and his radio close behind.

Screams of agony were heard intermittently from the enemy across the wire. Their wounds were no less painful than those of the Marines. Their blood ran the same color as the Marines. The cries for "corpsman" indicated there were wounded in the American camp as well.

As morning came and the fighting ended, the tally was three Marines from the artillery battery wounded by incoming. Fortunately, there were no Marine KIA's. All the wounded were medevaced and expected to survive.

The "shitter" on the hill was also hit, but would undergo repairs so that necessary business could resume. A patrol sent outside the perimeter brought in five bodies. From their uniforms, four were determined to be main force VC. The fifth was an NVA, probably an advisor to the VC.

Division took a particular interest in that firefight. So did Air America. A black and white Huey landed and non-uniformed Americans searched and photographed the bodies. The Marines knew Air America was a front for the CIA...who were they kidding?

Another supply chopper came that day. The men were treated to large institutional-size cans of peaches. There were enough cans so that every two men could share one, but one can could have easily fed an entire squad.

The men enjoyed those peaches like they were steak, but the next day, they paid for their indulgence. Henceforth it was called the "peach-shit," anticipated but worth the pain.

* * * * * *

Max received another letter from Sally. Her letters seemed more and more shallow. She wrote on and on about things he thought were meaningless. Nothing of her feelings, none of her dreams.

He wanted to read about *them*, about a future, about her feelings and fears. Maybe Sally had a new boyfriend. He remembered encouraging her to date while he was gone. Now, he was jealous. Viet Nam had made him lose his mind.

That's it, he concluded, she's dating someone and is writing just to be polite. He was in a bad mood when he wrote a stinging letter back.

Perhaps all the better, he rationalized. Sally came from a wealthy West Virginia family and had a strong religious upbringing. He always felt that if they did marry someday, her family would have a difficult time accepting him due to differences in familial status and religious denomination. Maybe it wasn't true, but that's the way he felt.

Max grew up the oldest of five children in a poor but close-knit blue-collar family whose lack of money was only an inconvenience. His parents were very traditional and had high values and the kids were brought up to be respectful and have a high degree of integrity.

Several days passed. As First Platoon was about to go on another patrol, PFC Jackson requested he be transferred to the Second Platoon so he could be with his best buddy. Since Lt. Larsen has no objections, Max left Jackson behind to be with the Second Platoon.

When Max and the patrol returned that evening, PFC Jackson was dead. It happened that Jackson and his buddy, PFC Wilson, were cleaning their weapons when Wilson, a grenadier who also carried a .45 automatic, had an accidental discharge of the .45. The bullet struck Jackson in his neck. He died on the medevac chopper before reaching the NSA hospital in Danang.

Dawson and Corbett kept to themselves. Corbett, whose cast was off, remained on light duty while Dawson could always find a reason not to go on patrol. Of the time Max spent on disciplinary matters, ninety percent of it was on those two.

Once Dawson protested he couldn't go on patrol because someone had "stolen" his rifle. A search quickly turned up the missing M-16 buried in the ground next to his gear. Max threatened to have him court-martialed if there was another offense.

Corbett constantly complained about his pain in his ankle and how the work details Max put him on were aggravating his condition.

On the fifty-sixth day at Thuong Duc, Kilo Company was scheduled to be sent back to Battalion for a few days rest before its next operation. The CH-46's landed on the LZ almost at the same time as the incoming rocket rounds. Some Marines were able to board as the first two helicopters abruptly lifted from the hot LZ.

One Marine fell off the loading ramp from a height of about ten feet. He was hurt, but not too bad. The rocket rounds originated from the village of Chan Son to the north. The 105's and 155's went to work and silenced the incoming, but not before two Marines lay dead.

One was Captain Newbury, his legs scathed at the hip. Ironically, the captain who was so concerned with his own safety that he never left the hill during the previous fifty-six days was dead.

The other KIA was a corporal from the Third Platoon. Eight other men were wounded, some critically. One Marine suffered the traumatic amputation of both legs above his knees. As Max did what he could to help, he found another of the wounded, also from the Third Platoon, his right leg almost completely severed above the knee. The dangling appendage was bent backwards beneath him exposing the shattered end of the femur. Lieutenant Cullen was with the corpsman by the Marine's side.

The choppers again landed and took out the wounded and dead first. Captain Newbury's body was wrapped in a poncho. Max had ambivalent feelings about Newbury's death. He hated the man for sending platoons out to do a company's job. He hated him for all those hellish three-day patrols. He hated him for his sneering attitude and for not looking after his men as an officer should.

Yet, as he watched his mutilated remains loaded on the helicopter, he felt sorry for him. Captain Newbury did all he could to survive at Thuong Duc. He only had a few weeks to go before he was headed home to his family. He felt sorrier for Newbury's family then he did for Newbury.

Max and the remainder of the First Platoon were last to board the choppers. As the bird lifted skyward, the last sight that caught his eye was the splintered box with the hole in the middle, on top of the hill.

CHAPTER 8

Down Under

Moree was a small town of less than ten-thousand inhabitants situated about two-hundred and seventy miles north and slightly west of Sydney, but still not as far north as Queensland.

The cottage they stayed in was small and contained only the bare essentials. Amber spent two entire days cleaning just to make it habitable. Their relationship was barely okay from the beginning. Gordon often went to town with his friends to drink and carouse, leaving her home alone. Some days were worse than others, but the nausea along with being left alone at night, made her life miserable. One evening she summoned the courage to face his sullen mood.

"Gordon, please don't go drinking with your mates again tonight... stay with me," she pleaded.

"Don't you be telling me what to do, girl," he said with a snarled lip. "I'll drink with anyone I damn bloody well feel like drinking with, and whenever I feel like drinking."

Amber became more and more despondent. Several weeks later, during another confrontation with Gordon, she was more shocked than physically hurt when he struck her with the back of his hand.

She rationalized his abuse as an isolated, alcohol-induced incident. But the abuse continued. Once she hit him back and he blackened her eye. When he came home drunk and demanded sex, she was disgusted. If she refused, he beat her.

Another time, she talked of leaving. He told her he would kill her if she tried to go anywhere. She became desperate not only for herself, but for the welfare of the baby. Now five and a half months pregnant, she didn't think she or the baby could take any more abuse. She despised Gordon. But her hatred was only superseded by her fear. She began to plan an escape.

With only the clothes on her back, she rode into town with Hawker, the hired cook on the ranch. They were intending to go food shopping. "Hawker, how well do you know Gordon?" she asked.

"Well enough to wonder why a pretty little miss like you is keeping his company."

"Tell me what you know, Hawker, please."

"I shouldn't be running my mouth missy. That Hamilton chap can be quite a handful if he is crossed."

"I have bruises to confirm that," she said.

"He's struck you then, has he?" Hawker asked.

"More than once, but never again."

"Look, I don't want no trouble from Hamilton, but I will tell you he got run out of Queensland."

"Do you know why, Hawker?"

"The boys, when they are drinking, talk a bunch, you know. Well, this one time around Christmas last year, Hamilton shows up just after he got run out. Seems he was bragging to the boys about how he was carrying on this affair with the ranch owner's wife."

"Was that it?"

"No ma'am, that ain't half it," Hawker continued. "Seems while he's fooling around with the Mrs., Hamilton's got him a wife of his own up in Darwin. Left her with two youngsters to care for. Anyway, the rancher finds out about his wife carrying on with Hamilton, and they get into it. Finally, he pulls a gun on Hamilton and runs him off his land. Hamilton sneaks back to the barn late that same night and slits the throat of the man's prize stallion."

Amber sat there dumbfounded. "He's married?" she murmured.

"I'm sorry, but I'm afraid it's true. He used to beat her up pretty good too. Even bragged about it."

"Hawker, as far as anyone knows, you didn't tell me anything, okay?"

"I'd appreciate that. Like I said, I don't want no trouble from Hamilton."

Hawker went into the market while Amber pretended to be waiting in the truck. She knew there was no way she could go back.

If I call home, John or Father would come for me. But no, with what she'd learned, it wasn't only humiliating to admit how right her brother had been, it might be deadly for him. No, she reasoned, it would be best if she just laid low for a while.

Forty-five minutes later she was on the bus for Sydney. It took all the money she had to buy her fare.

Later that afternoon, while walking the streets of Sydney, cold and hungry, she sadly and reluctantly pawned her only valuable, a small diamond and emerald locket set in eighteen-carat gold on a gold chain. Her parents had given her the necklace for her sixteenth birthday and she cherished it dearly but she was desperate.

It was late July and winter in the southern hemisphere. While not bitter cold, she would need to find shelter for the night. As night fell, she got caught up in her despair. Exhausted and despondent, she sat on a bench and cried. Reflecting back upon her circumstances, she could hardly believe how stupid she was to get involved with Gordon in the first place. John was so right. Gordon was no good. Behind that captivating smile of his was a deceitful, conniving, abusive bastard.

"Now things can't be all that bad, can they?" the woman's voice asked.

Amber nodded. "Right now, it's bad."

"Mind if I sit down a spell?"

Amber didn't say anything, but she slid over slightly.

"I'm Oli. Actually, my name is Olivia, but my friends call me Oli".

Amber looked at Oli for the first time. The woman looked to be in her early twenties, had short black hair and large dark brown, almost-black eyes. She was hard looking, yet there seemed a certain gentleness to her eyes, almost a sad gentleness, like those of a newborn calf.

"Do you have a name?" Oli asked.

"I'm sorry. I'm Amber... Amber McEwen".

"I see you're with child, Amber. Did you have a quarrel with your old man"?

"I don't have an old man. I don't have a husband. I don't have a boyfriend, and right now I don't even have a place to spend the night."

"Sounds pretty bad. Where are you from?" Oli asked.

"My home is down south, but I can't go back there now. I just got to Sydney today on the bus."

"Look, I got a flat a few blocks from here. It ain't much, but the roof don't leak and the water's hot. Why don't you let me put you up a spell?"

"No, I couldn't..." her words were cut off before she could finish.

"Yes you can. Now come along before we start to stick to this cold bench."

They were leftovers, but the food tasted good. The hot tea warmed the girls inside while their conversation, which lasted half the night, warmed their friendship.

Amber liked Oli. Each girl told her story, and while Amber thought she had a rough time, her plight was nothing compared to Oli's.

* * * * * *

Oli had grown up in Melbourne. Her parents had been killed in a tragic automobile accident when she was eight years old. She'd been sent to live with her aunt and uncle.

Her uncle was her father's half-brother and an alcoholic who beat his wife. When her aunt died about two years later, he began to sexually abuse Oli. One night, when she was thirteen years old, her uncle came home drunk, raped her, and passed out. Oli gathered her belongings, took whatever money of her uncle's she could find, and left. She ended up in Sydney, working, scrounging, even begging just to get by. But she survived.

Amber had never met a prostitute before, but she liked Oli regardless. Oli let her stay at her flat temporarily while Amber looked for work. In a couple of days, she found a job working in the kitchen of a restaurant. As time passed and Amber came closer to having her baby, Oli convinced her to stay with her and have the baby there. And, Oli knew of a midwife who could assist in the delivery.

Amber worked at the restaurant until into her ninth month when working became impossible. In the early morning hours of November 15, she gave birth to a healthy baby girl she named Amy.

In a few weeks, Amber returned to her job, and "Aunt Oli", who worked at her profession mostly nights, cared for Amy during the day. Oli always took her "customers" to a place her "manager" set up for his girls.

Life settled into a routine. Amber loved her daughter dearly and was supporting both of them, but barely. By now she was homesick and missed her family terribly. And, she missed Sunrise. She also missed her horse Tuffy and galloping across the open terrain. At last she decided to call home.

* * * * * *

Delia answered. Though Amber hadn't talked to her mother in over eight months, she told her all about Amy. She told her she was well and happy, even though that wasn't exactly the truth. She omitted some of the details, including the fact that Gordon had hit her, was married and that she'd left him. She also decided against telling her mother that she was living with a hooker.

The tone of her mother's voice was shaken. Instinctively, Amber knew something was terribly wrong. "What is it mother? How are Daddy and John?"

There was silence for a moment that seemed much longer. "Why didn't you call or write sooner? Why didn't you let us know where you were, that you were all right?"

"I couldn't, that's all. Perhaps I'll explain later."

"Your father is dead, Amber. He died three months ago from a heart attack. He was so lost without you. Every day he would say his little girl would be home soon. But you never came, and he will never see you again."

"Father is dead?" Amber said as her heart broke into pieces. "He can't be! Tell me it's not true, please mother, tell me it isn't so!" Tears ran down her cheeks unchecked.

"It is true, he is gone. John is running the ranch now."

Amidst the tears and overwhelming grief, Amber couldn't carry on the conversation with her mother. "I have to go now mother. I love you," she cried and then hung up the phone.

Amber clutched her daughter to her breast as she rocked back and forth on the edge of the bed, crying and mourning the loss of her father. And bearing the guilt of knowing her leaving had helped to kill him.

Amy began to fuss and stiffen her little arms and legs. Amber relaxed her embrace and through her tears, tried to soothe her infant.

* * * * * *

It was a quiet and lonely Christmas. Amber, "Aunt Oli" and Amy spent the holiday in the flat. They exchanged a few presents and had decorated a small tree mostly with items they had at hand. Amber had never been away from Sunrise on Christmas before. How she wished she could return there and see her father again.

The restaurant owner, a burly man in his forties, was becoming an increasing annoyance. Now that she was no longer pregnant and had her alluring body back, he started handling her.

In the beginning he would take "no" for an answer, but he became more and more aggressive as time went by. One day after closing, when all the other help had left, he cornered her in the kitchen and grabbed hold of her. She struggled as he tried to kiss her and fondle her at the same time. Working one arm free, she reached for a long-handled spatula and smacked him with it on the side of his head. He released his grasp.

The last thing she heard as she fled through the kitchen door, was "you're fired!"

CHAPTER 9

Kilo Company, Vietnam

There were no front lines in the Vietnam War. It was difficult to distinguish between the civilian populace and the enemy. Often times they assimilated within the same village.

Patrols went out and patrols came back, usually. Sometimes entire patrols were ambushed and wiped out. Other times, a single, large booby-trap, such as a 105mm artillery round would lay waste to an entire squad. Snipers were another ominous contention for the infantryman.

For the ensuing three months following Thuong Duc, Kilo Company, now under the command of Captain Pete Mitchell operated in and around the Danang and Dai Loc area to the south of Danang. Captain Mitchell was an admirable officer. Wounded, he had just returned from a hospital stay in Japan in time to fill the slot left by the late Captain Newbury. A Southerner from Tennessee, Pete Mitchell was about 5'10" tall, medium build, with closely cropped sandy blond hair and blue eyes. Only the cigars he smoked added some years to his boyish appearance.

Nevertheless, Max took an instant liking to the genteel captain, as did the other men of Kilo Company.

For perhaps a dozen consecutive nights, First Platoon was assigned night ambushes in a ville south of Danang. The VC had been known to pass through that ville at night, so Max and his platoon entered before dark and sat in an ambush along the perimeter.

At first the people of the village closed themselves in their hooches, but after several nights they became more trusting of the Marines and started leaving their doors open.

Max used the rustic front porch of one house as his command post. He made a concerted effort to befriend the people who lived there. They were a nice family. They had a daughter about sixteen years of age and two boys, perhaps ten and twelve.

To honor the Vietnamese custom of paying respect to the man of the house with gifts to distribute, Max brought candy bars for the children, a few cans of c-rations for the woman of the house and cigars for the man, giving all the gifts to the papa-san.

Before long, Max was invited inside the house during the long nights. The room off the porch was separate from the sleeping area. It was essentially bare except for a wooden table with chairs and an oil lamp upon the table that made for a decent place to write letters or to read.

The family kept a radio tuned to a Vietnamese station that played Vietnamese music until they went to sleep, usually around 2200, or ten PM. The music had a certain twang to it and in a way sounded like old country western music sung in Vietnamese and played as a 78 record on 45 and it made Max crazy. After the family went to sleep, Max enjoyed the nights, sitting at the table by the oil lamp.

One night he thought about Sally. He contemplated writing a letter of apology for the scathing letter he'd written her, but didn't. Instead, he wrote a letter home and then one to a good friend. Another all-nighter lay ahead.

It was about 0200 when it was his turn to man the radio which was set up on the porch. The squads were in position for the night. He had walked the lines earlier as they settled in. At approximately 0240, he ran a radio check of the squads.

"Kilo One Alpha, Kilo One Alpha, this is Kilo One."

"Kilo One, this is Kilo One Alpha, got you Lima Charlie," meaning they heard him loud and clear.

Max continued. "Kilo One Bravo, Kilo One Bravo, this is Kilo One, over."

"Kilo One, Kilo One Bravo, got you Lima Charlie."

"Kilo One Charlie, Kilo One Charlie, this is Kilo One." No response.

Max's heart skipped two beats. "Kilo One Charlie, Kilo One Charlie, this is Kilo One." Still no response. He tried a third time. The radio was silent.

Max knew that entire units had been killed in their sleep by the VC. He couldn't swallow around the lump in his throat. He cleared it twice before keying the mic again.

"Kilo One Alpha, Kilo One Alpha, Kilo One. Break. Kilo One Bravo, Kilo One Bravo, Kilo One."

"Alpha here."

"Bravo here."

"Be advised, I have no radio contact with one Charlie. Alert your men that Kilo One Actual is moving through the ville to Charlie's position."

"Lieutenant, you want me to go with you?" asked Corporal Shane.

"No, you stay here. Wake up Sgt. Gorman and Sgt. Ualena. If you don't hear from me in, say, eight minutes, come looking with the rest of the platoon. Got it?"

With that, Max chambered a round in his .45 and started for the west side of the ville, a distance of about forty yards traversing through the village around hootches, through a hedgerow, a large clump of banana trees, and through the old granny mama-san's garden.

It was dark and he dared not use a flashlight. The shadows took on a forboding veneer. Slowly, carefully, and as soundless as humanly possible, he came nearer the third squad's position.

He paused. and listened. He heard only the sounds of the black night and his own heartbeat.

A few more yards, and he spotted the shapes of men. He felt his heard pounding. A little closer. Closer yet. Now he could see the men still had their gear. He saw rifles.

"Damn," he hissed, his temper rising as his heartbeat regained a normal beat. *The whole fucking squad asleep in an ambush!* He walked among the men.

There was the radio, its volume turned low and an occasional muffled hissing sound emanating above the squelch. PFC Parker was on radio watch. He slept on his back, the handset only inches from his left ear. Just to his right slept Cpl. Garrison. Max kicked Garrison as he slept. Garrison set up, startled. Max stood over him with his finger over his mouth motioning Garrison not to speak and pointing two fingers towards his eyes, motioned Garrison to look around and see his squad all asleep, knowing instantly even in his grogginess, the seriousness of the situation.

Max then picked up Parker's poncho, threw it over Parker's head and simultaneously sat on him and commenced choking him long enough for Parker to get the message, but not succumb to cardiac arrest. Then he removed the poncho from Parker's head and stood up. Parker jolted to an erect position, his eyes as wide as baseballs. Max turned and left to return to his CP. Not a word was spoken.

Later that morning after the platoon moved out of the village, Corporal Garrison approached his platoon commander. "Lieutenant, you gonna have Parker court martialed for sleeping on watch?"

"Why should he be the *only* one, Corporal, that is, if I was to have him court martialed?"

"Well Sir, after you left, Parker was so scared he volunteered to man the radio the rest of the night. He said there was no way in hell he could go to sleep if he wanted to. You scared him so bad he shit on himself. I think Parker learned his lesson, Sir."

"Parker's a good troop. I have no intention of court martialing him or anyone else in the platoon, except maybe Dawson if he doesn't straighten up. I noticed he was blowing zee's like everyone else. Was he supposed to be awake?"

"Yes, Sir, he was. And thanks, Lieutenant. Parker will be glad to hear that."

"Corporal Garrison."

"Yes, Sir?"

"See that your squad maintains a fifty percent alert in all ambushes from now on."

"Yes, Sir."

Back in Battalion the next day, Max was awakened from his short nap by an explosion. It wasn't outgoing.

Then he heard the cries of anguished men. He grabbed his cartridge belt and bolted towards the area. The first man he saw, a black Marine, was on his back with his blood-soaked hands grasping his intestines which protruded from his abdomen. As Max knelt beside him, the Marine moaned, then gasped and expired.

Everywhere he looked, Max saw bleeding men. One man was so badly dismembered that only his dog tags would reveal his identity. Dangling from one of the guy-ropes of the tent was part of a human brain, which, only moments earlier was intact within the skull of a now-dead Marine.

Several corpsman were on the scene. At least eight men were dead, many more wounded. The medevac choppers were called in. Some of the wounded were carried directly to the BAS where the navy doctor worked on the more seriously wounded.

Still bloody from assisting the corpsman with battle dressings, Max went over to the mess tent for coffee. He sat there dazed at what he had just witnessed. The enemy didn't kill those men, they were killed by the careless action of one man. While piecing together the mangled bodies, Max heard bits and pieces of the tragedy. Lima Company had come off patrol when one of the men, now among the deceased, had dumped a tee-shirt full of patrol-collected grenades onto a cot. Apparently a pin dislodged, causing the spontaneous explosion and subsequent senseless death and maiming of too many young men.

Max shook his head. The Marine Corps didn't like to tell families their loved ones had died under such circumstances. More than likely, the families of the deceased would be told that while Lance Corporal, or Private First Class, or whoever, was killed in action by enemy fire. *All the better.* Max sighed, then sipped at his coffee.

"Lieutenant?...Lieutenant? Are you all right, Sir?"

"Oh, Sgt. Ualena, I'm sorry, I was just thinking. Care for some coffee?"

"Thank you, Sir, but I have some mail to distribute. You got two letters yourself."

"Thanks, Sarge."

I'll be damned, Max thought as he opened the first letter, the one from Sally Garfield.

I know it must be very difficult for you there in Vietnam. The news reports are horrible. There are so many men dying there. Do you still believe it is all worth it? The letter continued. *Max, I almost did not send this letter. I was not sure after your last letter that you even wanted to hear from me but I decided to send it anyway. Do you remember when we talked about meeting in Hawaii on your R&R? Well,* Sally continued, *I don't think that is a good idea anymore. Besides, my parents did not approve of my going anyway. I don't know if I will hear from you again, if that's what you want. If not, please take care of yourself. We had lots of good times and I will always remember you. Love, Sally.*

Shit. Max shook his head and fought the urge to crush the paper in his fist. He took a deep breath and stared at the letter he'd laid on the table. A new weariness settled into his soul. *Why am I so bitter?*

Was it Sally, or the war? Maybe neither. *War sure sucks.* He'd seen things in a few short months that he would never have imagined possible. His idealistic preaching to Sally and other friends about supporting the government? *What the hell was that?* The politicians wouldn't give them permission or equipment to win the fucking war. They just kept sending young man into the battle to be bloodied, crushed, killed.

His laugh was harsh. Maybe all that bullshit was just a way to rationalize and justify an opportunity to prove his manhood.

Hawaii, he thought, as he looked at the blood splattered on his hands and clothes. *Fuck it, I don't want to go to Hawaii anyway.*

It was now December and he was tired. After seven months of combat, fatigue had taken its toll. He was beginning to feel total exhaustion. Periodically, he learned of classmates from OCS who had been killed. Franklin, Hank Long, Bill Lindsey...all dead. He picked up a copy of the Stars & Stripes.

George Anderson, the lieutenant he'd met his first day in Nam, was among the KIA's. In his own platoon, PFC Parker, who'd survived Max's mock attack after he fell asleep on watch was now dead from a sniper round to his head.

Lance Corporal Sealy, dead from a booby-trapped grenade. Lance Corporal Shipley, sent home minus his left arm and his legs from the knees down. The list seemed endless.

* * * * * *

Captain Mitchell was not immediately receptive to Max leaving on R&R. "We're heading out on another major operation in a couple of days," the skipper said. "I sure could use you."

"Skipper, I've been at this twenty four hours a day, seven days a week for seven months now. I need a break. Besides," Max went on, "I'll only be gone a week."

Pete Mitchell knew Max was right. The Captain could see it in Max's sunken eyes and hear it in his voice. Max wasn't begging, but in his own way, almost pleading from his heart. Besides, if Max was beat, the Company couldn't fully depend on him. He nodded at Max.

"Go on then. Have a good time, Lieutenant."

"Thanks, Skipper."

"Oh, and by the way, don't catch the clap," the Captain said with a smile.

Max nodded and smiled back.

CHAPTER 10

R & R Sydney, Australia, December 1968

The Chevron Hotel was located in Kings Cross, a suburb of Sydney. It was the hotel used as the headquarters for the R&R coordinators. Servicemen flew to their R&R destinations in uniform but were not to remain in uniform once there. At the Chevron, local merchants rented civilian clothing on a weekly basis.

Upon arrival, Max rented a few shirts, a pair of shoes, a sport jacket, a couple pair of dress slacks and a few ties. He also took a room at the Chevron since it was well located.

Kings Cross was the happening place. It was great to be back in civilization. Before leaving the hotel room, Max laid down on the bed—the first bed he'd laid on in over seven months—but only briefly, for he thought he might sleep the whole week away. He walked into the bathroom...a real flush toilet—the first he'd sat on in the same amount of time.

Cars, stores, restaurants...how much we take for granted. He stopped for lunch. Cold beer...what a luxury! And girls! As he scanned the area, he saw more beautiful women then he had seen in almost a year.

The war was horrific, but for a week it could be temporarily forgotten—and he'd be damned busy enjoying life's pleasures.

Lieutenant Mike Cullen, who had previously taken his R&R in Sydney, had told Max about the "Rathskeller", a true Down Under bar where the beer flowed and the girls "were accommodating."

When Max arrived, it was only mid afternoon. What the hell, he thought, let the party begin. The bar was actually below street level, in a basement. The place wasn't very large, the music was loud, and the crowd lively. It wasn't packed, but it was busy.

Most of the men in the place looked like GI's, but some, considering the accent, were Australian or New Zealander's. A few GI's were quite drunk. One was staggering up the stairway to the street with his arm around the girl who was helping him..

Max had heard that the Aussie women loved American servicemen because they treated them better than the Aussie men did.

"What'll it be, mate?" asked the barmaid. She was kind of cute herself, although a little on the short and plump side.

"I'd like a beer, cold and in a bottle."

"We have Four X, Fos..." she started to name the brands when Max cut her off.

"Cold, in a bottle, any Aussie beer will be fine."

"Be right back," she said with a smile.

As he sat in the booth downing his second, he couldn't keep the flashbacks of Vietnam away. Here he was, thousands of miles from the war, yet being in Australia seemed like light-years away. He finished a third beer and then left.

On his way back to the Chevron he felt good. The beer just mellowed him enough. It was December, summer in the southern hemisphere, and the warm, sunny day was pleasant, not oppressive as in Nam. Three girls stood along the sidewalk, two of them leaning against the building. The third girl, who was not leaning against the building was more aggressive in her pursuit of business.

"Hey, you want to go?" she asked in her distinct accent.

He was aware of the prostitutes in Sydney, and while they were not bad looking women, Max didn't feel he would be so unfortunate this week so as to have to pay for the services rendered. He declined the solicitation.

It was late afternoon, and back at the hotel he crawled nude between the sheets for a nap, the comfort of the bed in the air-conditioned room was like no other luxury he could recall.

It was almost two hours later when he awoke. After showering and getting dressed, he headed for a local restaurant that had been recommended. He ate alone, thoroughly enjoying the fine dinner; a delicacy after living on c-rations for the past seven months.

* * * * * *

The cab driver suggested the Starlight Club in downtown Sydney so Max readily agreed. It was a large, glitzy club with a live band and dancers in cages on either side of the stage. It was crowded.

There was a girl, apparently alone, sipping a drink through a small cocktail straw. He approached.

"Hi, mind if I join you?"

"You're American," she said.

"So are you, it seems."

"You on R&R?"

"How can you tell? Is my rented jacket a giveaway?" Max said with a smile.

She laughed. "No, it's your haircut. Besides, most of the guys here are Americans on R&R."

"I'm Max Elliot."

"Colleen Douglas. Nice to meet you, Max."

"What do you know, I come all the way to Australia and the first girl I meet is from the U.S."

"Is there something wrong with that?" she asked.

"No, not really," Max replied. "It's just a little ironic, that's all. What are you doing here anyway? You're not in the service are you?"

"No," she answered. "I came to Australia to work, over a year and a half ago. Things just haven't gone for me as I anticipated. Now, all I want to do is save up enough money to buy a plane ticket home."

"Where is home?" he asked.

"Baltimore." Colleen paused. Her smile was gone and her eyes were incredibly sad. "I guess I'm just really homesick. I can't wait to get out of Australia."

Max decided he needed to politely get himself away. The last thing he needed was a somber American girl in distress. "Well, Colleen, it was nice meeting you. I think I'll walk around some. I'm still a little stiff from the nine-hour flight down here. Hope you get to go home soon."

"Did I scare you off that bad?" she said.

"No. No you didn't. But I just got here today. Maybe I'll see you around." With that, Max parted, breathing a sigh of relief.

With another cold Fosters in hand, Max walked around the outer edge of the dance floor away from Colleen and watched people dance. While eyeing a trim, pretty, blue-eyed blonde with short hair, he had seemed to catch her eyes as well. The music briefly stopped. Max made his move.

"Care to dance?" he asked.

"Sure," she said.

"I'm Max, and you?"

"I'm Susan."

And did she ever have that Aussie accent! "I guess I'm a little rusty with my dancing, "Max said. "Haven't had much opportunity the past seven months."

"You just in from Nam?" she asked.

"You can tell, can't you?"

The music stopped. "Let's just say your accent tells me you're American and your haircut tells me you're probably a Marine."

"You're good at this. I guess you meet a lot of guys like me here, don't you?"

"I like to have fun. And that's what you guys are here for, isn't it?"

Bingo! *Now this is the kind of girl I want to meet.* "Susan, let's have fun."

They danced. They drank. And they did have fun. At one point, while slow dancing, Max caught a glimpse of Colleen standing alone near the dance floor. She was watching him, but he quickly took his eyes off her, hoping she did not see him notice her.

Max and Susan left together about 2:00 AM. "In the U.S. it is customary for a guy to escort a lady home," he said.

"I'd like that." she said. "I have my own flat. It's only a few blocks walk from here."

They talked as they walked along in the breezy but warm night air. Max felt great in spite of his head buzzing from the beer. He hadn't kept count, but he must have drank at least a six pack and then some. It was still hard for him to believe he wasn't in Vietnam. There were none of the sounds of war...no outgoing artillery...no incoming rounds from the enemy...no sounds of gunfire in the night...and to wear civilian clothes again, with no helmet or flak jacket. Best of all it was great to be clean and smell good.

At the door, Max kissed her goodnight. "Won't you come in?" she asked.

"Sure."

It wasn't long before they both got what they wanted.

Susan moaned softly as Max thrust into her body.

He nearly clawed the plaster from the wall above the bedframe when he reached an orgasm simultaneously with hers.

The following day, he took Susan sailing aboard a chartered 65' cutter in Sydney harbor and included a barbecue lunch on a beach. The dinghy towed behind the sailboat ferried the few couples aboard to the remote beach while the cutter lay at anchor in the secluded cove. Susan had a deep tan and a gorgeous body that fit nicely into her skimpy, floral-patterned pink and turquoise bikini.

They had dinner later that night at a fine seafood restaurant that Susan recommended. Max ate lobster, his favorite. That night they stayed together at the Chevron and enjoyed the pleasure of each other's body. They were good together, but the chemistry was more physical than mental, and they both knew it.

The following day they went to Bondi Beach, a beautiful crescent-shaped beach with soft white sand adorned with thousands of beachgoers. But after the beach, Max didn't make any plans with her for that evening. He sensed she was probably a little hurt, but he wanted to be free to see what would unfold.

He asked Susan to drop him off in Kings Cross. He then walked the two blocks to the Rathskeller and went in for a beer. There weren't many patrons present. A buxom girl with short, probably-dyed black hair and dark eyes sat down next to him.

"Hi, I'm Jodi."

"I'm Max."

"You were here the day before yesterday, weren't you?" she asked.

Max hadn't noticed her before. "Yeah, I was here for a couple of beers."

"You looked lonely. I didn't want you to be lonely again today."

"Well, actually when I was in here two days ago I had just gotten into town."

"You're a yank Marine, are you?"

"I suppose you could say that," Max answered when suddenly he remembered Mike Cullen telling him about this girl, Jodi, he had picked up at the Rathskeller. "Do you know a Marine lieutenant who was here about a month ago—his name is Mike Cullen?"

Jodi's eyes grew large and her nostrils flared. "He's a goddamned pig!" she exclaimed. "Why, is he a friend of yours?"

Actually, Mike *was* a friend. He'd told Max about a girl named Jodi who would do anything in bed, and he'd boasted about how they did this and that, but Mike was obviously not standing in high esteem with the lady present at the table.

"Oh, uh, we serve in the same unit in Nam, and he told me about this place."

"So Jodi, what do you do?" Max asked quickly and moreover to change the subject.

"I do this," she said.

"You do what? You hang out in bars and drink?" Max asked.

"Yeah, that's what I do; I hang out in bars and drink. Is there something wrong with that?" she questioned with consternation.

"No...oh no." Max said. "I think that's a fine career."

The time passed and the beer bottles covered the table top when they left the bar together. Back at the room at the Chevron, everything Mike said was true. Jodi was uninhibited in bed. They slept about an hour after their interlude. Max woke first and looked at the body beside him. Her skin was slightly clammy and her hair smelled from smoke. Her scent resembled that of the Rathskeller.

She stirred, then woke, and when she spoke, the latent beer breath only added to Max's desire to get rid of her. "Listen, I made plans earlier to meet someone, so I'm sorry we can't spend any more time together," Max said.

He'd never been a good liar, and no doubt he hadn't convinced her, either.

Jodi got out of bed, quickly dressed and paused as she was about to leave. Almost snarling, she glared at Max who remained propped up in the bed. "You're just like your goddamn friend!" she lashed out. "You buy a girl a few drinks, take her to bed and then you throw her out. Fuck you!" she said as she slammed the door behind her.

Max pondered the scene a few moments and wondered if he should feel bad for what he'd done. But just what did he do that he should feel bad about? He shrugged it off and hit the shower.

It was about five in the afternoon when he strolled along the sidewalk in Kings Cross. He wasn't hungry and it was too early to eat dinner anyway. A couple passed in the opposite direction, walking arm in arm. He paused at a store and window-shopped. As he continued walking, he felt mellow and for the first time in seven months he felt rested and relaxed. It had taken three days to unwind from the war.

As he ambled along, the shapely figure walking ahead caught his eye. The miniskirt only accentuated the curves, part of which included deeply tanned legs proportioned as if created by a master sculptor. The long dark hair bounced upon her back. He lengthened his stride until he was beside her. She looked at him over her left shoulder as soon as she was aware of his presence. Never had he seen such breathtaking green eyes or a face as equally alluring. She stopped. Max stopped.

His heart accelerated as she looked into his eyes and spoke before he had the chance. "You want to go?" she said with hesitation as if she didn't really mean it.

He couldn't believe such a beautiful woman was a whore, but his defenses liquefied like molten lava. He didn't have to think of what to say. The words rolled off his tongue.

"Yes, I do." He'd never felt so captivated by a woman's looks. It didn't matter that he'd just been solicited.

"Come with me," she said in a monotone, devoid of any feeling.

"I'm staying at the Chevron, why don't we go there?"

"No, you'll come with me."

"Listen, don't worry, I'll pay you," he emphasized."

She didn't immediately respond, and Max sensed she was contemplating his offer, but again she asserted her terms. The encounter was to take place at the location of her choosing. He followed her off the main street, up two flights of stairs and into a large dingy room divided into half a dozen cubicles on either side of a center aisle-way. Each cubicle offered the privacy of a curtain along its front.

"This way," she ordered, as if being led to a higher authority to face corporal punishment. He felt disgust at being in such a place. He felt equally disgusted at himself for being with a whore, something he never thought he would do.

As they walked down the center aisle to the last cubicle on the right, Max turned to see an old man leaving the adjacent cubicle.

He walked with a cane and was at least eighty years old. The scantily clad girl who had just provided the elderly gentleman with her services stood by the curtain and said cheerfully, "See you same time next week, Mr. Wimple."

Max's attention was called to the girl whose attraction brought him there. She was blunt. "Twelve dollars pants down, twenty dollars, stripped." It was matter of fact and strictly business for her. He felt a lump form in his chest, and yet....

"Here's twenty."

She undressed and lay on her back on the bed. "Get on with it," she commanded.

Max slipped off the loafers, removed his jeans and mounted her. He was gentle. He attempted to kiss her, but she purposely turned her face away.

"Are you done?" she asked.

He was, but the callousness of her nature and the lack of participation on her part, made the experience a big disappointment. Yet, as he watched her get dressed...observing her long, flowing dark hair silhouetted against the sunlit window behind her, he could not help being enamored by her beauty and puzzled by why such a compelling female would resort to prostitution.

He walked up to her and out of the direct sunlight where he could see the soft lines of her face, an inconsistency with her austere manner. "I want to see you again," he spoke, doubting his own judgment as the words rolled off his lips.

"Same terms second time around," she said staying consistent with her all-business attitude.

Max touched her hair. She grabbed his arm, but he still held her hair softly in his hand. He looked into her irresistible eyes. "Why are you so hard when you are so beautiful?" he asked.

"Listen, I don't do this because I like it *or* because I want to. I have a kid to support. Now I think you better be going."

Max sensed a sadness in her voice. Reluctantly, he left. He went for dinner alone, but didn't have much of an appetite. He was thinking about the girl whose name he didn't even know.

* * * * * *

The next day he searched the streets of Kings Cross, but to no avail. He questioned another hooker who either would not or could not tell him anything by description. He went back to the upstairs room where he had gone with her yesterday, but she wasn't there either.

This is crazy. Why am I wasting my precious time trying to find a whore when this city is full of gorgeous women just waiting for a good time with an American GI? But he couldn't help it. He tried telling himself he was no longer looking for her, when all he was doing was looking at every girl to see if it *was* her.

By mid afternoon, he figured she probably didn't start work until late afternoon or evening. He stopped at a sandwich shop for lunch. The waitress was taking his order when he noticed a cute child, about a year old and barely able to walk, standing in the aisle supporting herself by holding on to her mother's arm. The woman, who had been looking at the menu, turned her head revealing her profile. *It's her!*

As he approached the table, she looked at him. "I'm not working today, come back tomorrow."

"May I sit down?" he asked softly.

"Look, I have my daughter with me, and I told you I'm not working today. Why don't you leave me alone?" She spoke with the same harshness as he remembered, but there was a slight inflection of emotion, almost desperation, in her voice.

Max sat down. "I'm Max Elliot, what's your name?"

"You don't give up, do you?"

"Here's the deal, tell me your name and I'll buy lunch."

She studied him, but didn't reply.

"That's all, no strings attached. Just tell me your name and lunch is on me. Okay?"

Her eyes were now looking at her daughter. For a moment she didn't say anything, then she looked at Max again.

"Okay," she said.

"Well?" Max said.

"Well, what?" she barked.

"What's your name?"

"Oh, that," she said, and for the first time gave a hint of a smile revealing a glimpse of a live human being behind the formidable facade. "Amber," she said. "My name is Amber."

"Amber what?" Max pushed.

"You ask a lot of goddamn questions, you know that, Yank?"

"Take it easy. All I asked for was your name, that's all."

"What are you doing, taking a goddamned census?"

"Look, I'm sorry I upset you. I've only been here a few days. I've been in Vietnam the past seven months and haven't seen anyone as pretty as you in a long time. I'd like to know you, that's all."

"Seems you got to know me pretty well for twenty bucks, yesterday."

"That's not what I mean," Max said quietly.

"Oh, what the hell," she said. "Amber McEwen. Actually, it's Amber Dawn McEwen."

"That's a pretty name. And who do we have here?" Max asked as he looked at the child.

"This is my daughter, Amy." As she spoke, she picked Amy up onto her lap and kissed her cheek. "She's my life."

"I can see why," Max said. "She's as pretty as her mother. How old is Amy?"

"Almost thirteen months now."

"What'll it be miss?" the waitress asked.

Amber placed her order and Max had his brought to the same table. As they ate, Amber remained distant, but cordial.

"I have to go now," she said as she abruptly stood up and picked up her child. "Thanks for lunch."

"Where do I find you?" Max asked. "I want to see you again."

"I don't think that's a good idea," she answered.

"But why not?"

"Give it up, Yank!"

"I'll pay you. I'll pay you double, how's that?"

"Gawd, you yanks sure get horny, don't you?" she said. "I'll meet you tomorrow, by the apothecary on the corner, at four in the afternoon."

As she left, Max watched her until she was out of sight. Her tightly fitted jeans and the forest green top exposing her midriff left an impression in his mind that interfered with him having as good a time with Susan that night as he had with her previously. His obsession with Amber was consuming.

He was there at ten of, but she didn't arrive until four fifteen. "Let's go," she said with nigh a hint of compassion.

"No," Max said.

"What do you mean, no?" she said angrily. "Don't you want sex?"

"Not necessarily."

"What the hell is that suppose to mean?" she snarled with fists on her hips.

"I want to know who you are."

"I already told you yesterday who I am."

"That's not what I mean."

"Look Yank, you...

Max interrupted her. "My name's not Yank, it's Max. Call me Max, okay?"

"Look Max, I don't know what the hell you want from me, but I have to earn a living, so do you want to go or not?"

"We'll go, but not to that sleazy place you took me to yesterday. We're going to the Chevron."

Amber protested, but then relented. "All right, but only for one trick, and you pay up front."

She was obviously uncomfortable as she entered the hotel room. Max felt she hadn't gone to places other than that slimy upstairs flat do provide her services. "How about a glass of wine? That's all I have."

"Okay."

He handed her the wine and she took a sip before setting the glass down. He got close to her, put his arms around her waist and tried to kiss her, but her body stiffened like an icicle and she turned her cheek.

"No kissing and pay up first," she asserted.

Max knew the going rate—*twelve dollars pants down, twenty dollars stripped*. He handed her a hundred dollar bill. She looked at the money but didn't say anything. "Here, take it," he said.

"I don't have any change," she said.

"I don't want any change," he said.

"Just what the hell do you *want* for a hundred bucks?"

"You really want to know? I'll tell you. I want your company. I want to talk to you. I want to know what makes you tick. I want to know why you do what you do. I want to know everything about you." He paused before continuing. "I want to know that behind that tough facade there's a warm, loving, caring person. I watched you with your daughter. It's in there."

"You left out that you want to fuck me."

"I have to go back to Nam in a few days," Max said. "I want to spend those days with you. "I'll pay you well, more than you'll make on the street, but I don't want you to act like a hooker. I want you to act like a girl that met a guy on R&R and is out for a good time."

"I don't know about all this. I don't think I can do this."

"Yes you can. Again Max put his arms around her, but he didn't go any farther.

"What do you want me to do now?" she said.

"I want you to go home and get dressed for a really great dinner tonight. Meet me back here at seven."

"That's it. You're paying me a hundred bucks to have dinner with you? How do you know I won't just cut out and not come back?"

"I don't, but I'm hoping you'll come back."

It was almost seven-thirty when she knocked on the door. Max opened it. "I was beginning to have my doubts," he said.

"I wasn't coming at first, but I changed my mind. Are we going or staying?"

"We're going. I hope you're hungry."

"I'm starving."

She was obviously uncomfortable, but as the dinner progressed Amber began to open up, revealing very little about her past. She did say she shared a flat with a girl named Oli who also worked the streets. She said Oli took her in when she was desperate and had nowhere to go and that she came originally from a small town in the southern part of New South Wales. She was careful not to reveal very much about herself.

After dinner they went to a small club where they drank and danced. Max thought she appeared to be enjoying herself. Then he took her back to the Chevron. When they got into the room, she began to undress.

"There's no need for that," Max said.

Perplexed, Amber held her blouse up to her bare breasts. He put his arms around her and held her. Again she stiffened, almost as if she were preparing to be struck.

"Why are you so afraid?" Max asked.

"I don't want to be hurt anymore, that's all."

"I'm not going to hurt you," he said.

"Look Max, I don't want to get involved with anyone either. Besides, you'll be gone in a few days and there will be other yanks here."

"I don't want to think about where I'm going in three days. I only want to think about here and now. And now I know that I want to spend that time with you."

She sighed. He lifted her chin and kissed her softly. She didn't turn her cheek. "I'll take you home now."

Puzzled, Amber looked at him, as though not quite sure what to make of him. "That's it? I don't have to go to bed with you?"

"No, you don't," he said. "As I said, I'll take you home now."

"No, I don't want you taking me home. I'll go myself, but thanks, anyway." Amber turned to leave, then stopped, turned again towards Max, and kissed him. "Thanks," she whispered, then slipped out the door.

What is it about her that obsesses me? He wanted her so badly, and her body was his. He'd paid for her, but let her go. He desperately wanted to make love to her, but when he did, it would be more than sex. He wanted her to *want* to make love to him.

The next day Max, Amber and Amy went to Bondi Beach. They swam, built sand castles with Amy and enjoyed a wonderful day. "My manager wants to know where I was yesterday," Amber said.

Max propped himself on one elbow. "You mean your pimp, don't you?" He deeply regretted what he had just said, but it was too late.

"Look you bastard, you know goddamn well what I do, so don't be cutting me down now!"

"I'm sorry. What did you tell him?"

"It doesn't matter anyway. It's really none of your business."

"Let's forget it," Max said. "Look, Amy just smashed the castle. I guess she's protesting your outrage."

Amber laughed.

That evening they again went for a fine dinner. They spent four hours in the restaurant. This time Amber talked about growing up on the Sunrise and how a jackaroo named Gordon Hamilton turned her life into a shambles.

"But why didn't you go home when you left him?" Max asked.

"I was too headstrong and at the same time, ashamed. My parents and my brother all told me that Gordon was no good. I didn't listen to them. When finally I did leave Gordon and called home, I wanted desperately to return to the Sunrise."

"Why didn't you?"

"I learned my father had died. I felt responsible. I just couldn't go home, then." She held her head low and Max could see tears glistening on her eyelashes.

They went back to the Chevron. Max removed his wallet that contained almost seven hundred dollars in cash. He placed it on the nightstand by the bed. "I didn't pay you today," he said. "There's my wallet. I want you to spend the night with me, and in the morning, take whatever you need to take."

It was the best night he had ever had, anywhere, at any time, with anyone. Amber was warm and receptive, returning the physical love with a tenderness that was genuine. He held her, kissed her, and they made love. They also talked. She told him about her family and about the Sunrise, and about her horse, Tuffy. It was when she talked of home that her sadness was most noticeable.

"Why don't you go home?" Max asked gently.

"I can't. My mother and brother probably hate me," she said.

"Do they know what kind of work you've been doing here in Sydney?" Max asked.

"They don't even know I'm *in* Sydney," she replied. "They don't know where I am."

"What about the baby? Do they know about Amy?"

"They know I had her, that's all."

Max held her a little closer and she rolled over, putting her head on his chest. "How long have you been on the streets doing this?"

For a moment she didn't answer. "Not very long at all, actually. Oli took me in when I was desperate. She was really good to me. I even gave birth to Amy in her flat. I worked several different jobs, respectable ones at that, but every place I worked there was always a man who couldn't leave his hands off me.

"I would either quit or be let go for not cooperating, so to speak. A few months ago Oli got real sick; even went to the hospital for four days. She was laid up in bed for weeks and the money ran out—hers and mine." Amber cleared her throat and looked him in the eyes.

"Oli really didn't want me to go out on the streets, but we were in a bad way. I thought I would do it only long enough for her to get well again. The first night I asked a GI if he wanted to go, and I hoped he would say no. I was scared to death. When he said yes, I just told him to go to hell, and I ran off. The next day I went through with it. I hated doing it, and still do.

"What happened to Oli?" Max asked.

"She got better and went back to work. I just continued doing it. I felt if men were going to put their hands on me, I might as well get paid for it. But mostly, I've had time to raise Amy." Again she paused. "I have wondered these past few months if I would ever be capable of having a normal relationship with a man again."

"How do you feel with me?" Max asked.

"Sad," she said.

"Come on, I'm not *that* pathetic," Max jested.

"It's just that you've shown me I can be myself again, and now I'm afraid to go back on the streets."

He kissed her again, and they joined their bodies as one. The last thing Max remembered before falling off to sleep was how he loved touching her hair and how he loved her scent.

The early morning sun peaked through the curtains and he awoke. She was gone. "Damn!" His eyes caught his wallet on the nightstand. He opened it. All his cash was still in it. Then he saw the note on the small table by the window.

Dear Max, You've been wonderful. Thanks for making me feel human again. Amber.

On the streets he asked every girl he found if they knew Amber McEwen. One girl knew who she was but didn't know where she lived. It was hours later when he found a girl who knew Oli, and where she lived, which could lead him to Amber.

It was only about two miles away, but he took a taxi so he could get there as quickly as possible. The old lady who owned the house rented the flat upstairs to the girls. She didn't want to let Max in, but he ushered himself past her and bolted up the stairs, taking three steps at a time. He banged on the door.

"You must be that Marine. Max is it?" said Oli.

"Where is she," he said.

"She doesn't want to see you again."

"Where is she"! Max asserted, this time in his Lieutenant mode.

The voice came from behind Oli. "It's okay, Oli, let him in." Amber stood there, her dark hair draped over a light blue work shirt halfway unbuttoned and hanging loosely over her jeans. She was barefoot, and the tear that fell from her eye landed on her foot. Other tears had left their damp markings on her shirt. "You should not have come here," she said.

Max walked over to her as Oli stepped aside. He kissed the tears on her cheeks. "I'm not letting you go," he said.

With that came another burst of tears. "You're leaving tomorrow, damn you! Why did you have to come into my life?"

Softly, Max answered, "Yes, I am leaving tomorrow, but I'll get another R&R, and as soon as I finish my time in Nam, I'll be back for you."

Amber pulled away from him, confused, and ran her fingers through her hair. Then she turned towards him. "What am I suppose to do in the meantime?" she bemoaned.

"Get your shoes on and not waste anymore of the time we have left."

"Where are we going?"

"Horseback riding," he said.

Amidst the tears, Amber managed a smile. She had not been on a horse in almost a year now. "Where?" she asked.

"You'll see, get ready."

Amber turned to Oli, but Oli already knew what she was about to ask. "You go, Amy and I have things to do today."

Amber gave Oli a hug, then picked up Amy and kissed her.

* * * * * *

At the Chevron, Max had seen an advertisement for a ranch about sixty miles outside of Sydney that offered trail rides in the mountains. They even had transportation from the hotel and back. Max had ridden horses as a kid and loved it.

For Max, it was amazing beyond description. They saw kangaroo, koalas, and even a platypus, animals indigenous and unique to the continent. Amber was a natural in the saddle. He watched her as her hair blew in the wind as freely as the mane of her mount.

They cantered on the trail that led around the mountain and overlooked the draw and adjacent higher peak. The sweet air smelled of the lush mountain foliage. Max was galloping ahead when the large bay gelding stumbled and went down. He hit the ground and rolled several times before coming to a stop.

The horse got up, but Max didn't. Amber reined in, jumped from the mare and rushed to him. "Are you alright?" she cried.

Then he grabbed her and pulled her down, wrapping his arms around her and kissing her.

"You fool!" she exclaimed as she got up smiling. "Let's catch our horses before we have to walk back."

Back at the ranch station, they enjoyed a barbecue dinner before the van took them back to town.

That evening, Max's last night in Sydney, the two cherished and made the most of what little precious time they had left. It was a night like the previous night, only better. In the morning, they showered together before he put on his Marine uniform for the return journey to Vietnam. They had breakfast in the hotel and both avoided conversation pertaining to their inevitable parting. Max had to be ready to board the bus for the airport at 8:00 AM. They held hands as they walked outside to the bus.

Max handed Amber an envelope. "But I...." he cut her off.

"There's about six hundred dollars in here," he said. It was all the cash he had left. "I won't be needing it where I'm going and besides I get paid again when I get back. You're finished working the streets."

"Oh Max, I love you," she said as she put her arms around him and her head on his chest.

It was time to go. There was a final kiss and embrace. "Goodbye, Max."

"Don't say goodbye," he said. "Say, see you later. Goodbye sounds too permanent. I promise you, I'm coming back."

Max was the last to board the bus. It started moving when he got to a window near the back.

"See you later yank!" Amber yelled. "I love you!"

He yelled back, "I love you!" He watched her stand there until the bus turned the corner, then he slumped into the seat.

He was already missing her.

CHAPTER 11

Back in Hell

The screen door slammed behind Max as he dropped his valpack on the wooden deck of the hooch where First Sergeant Rucker lived and worked in the Battalion command post for 3/1.

"Hey Lieutenant, welcome back."

"Thanks Top, we win the war yet?"

"We sure did…kicked Charlie's ass all the way to Hanoi. We're all going home tomorrow, too!"

"Got anymore fairytales, Top?" Max asked.

"I hope you had a good R&R, Lieutenant."

"What's happened, Top?" Max asked, knowing from the first sergeant's voice and expression that something was wrong.

"The entire Battalion is now part of a multi-national operation. ARVN, Aussies, ROKS, we're all in it. The operation started three days ago. Op name is Taylor Common. Kilo is down in An Hoa. We've lost several men already. Mostly SFD's and snipers."

He was almost afraid to ask. "Any from First Platoon?"

"Sorry Lieutenant, but Corporal Garrison, PFC Keaton and Sergeant Ualena are KIA."

Max sat down hard on the empty shell-casing box used as a chair. The guilt was crushing him, making it hard to breath.

"Captain Mitchell said he needed me," he muttered. But would his presence have made a difference? Would those men be alive today if he had not taken R&R? All the euphoria he'd enjoyed the past week... was all gone. Sucked out of him in seconds.

But if he hadn't gone to Australia when he did, he may not have met Amber. Was it fate? Was there such a thing as fate? Was it his destiny to go on R&R when he did? Was it his destiny to meet a beautiful girl with green eyes in Sydney, Australia?

But more, was it Corporal Garrison, PFC Keaton and Sgt. Ualena's destiny to die on foreign soil in an unpopular war? He spoke sorrowfully. "Keaton was going home this week."

He remembered the time Keaton was stung by a giant hornet while they were on patrol on Charlie Ridge. Keaton had a lump on the back of his head the size of a lemon. He was on the ground in pain and wanted to be air lifted but Max couldn't see calling in a medevac for a bee sting, so he told Keaton to get up and start walking or he would leave him there for the VC. Keaton got up and started walking. Of course, there was no way in hell he would have left him there.

"Sergeant Ualena, he has a wife and two kids back home in Hawaii. Corporal Garrison was a short timer. He only had a few weeks to go." Max stared at the floor when the first sergeant, caring and no doubt feeling the same sentiments, spoke.

"Lieutenant, you better get your gear ready. The skipper needs you out there. There's a chopper gonna fly out there in about thirty minutes. You need to be on it."

There was no transition period between R&R and Vietnam, between war and peace, life and death, sanity and insanity, civilization and third world decadence. A nine hour plane ride was all there was to separate making love to one human being and killing another.

Pete Mitchell welcomed Max's return to the bush. Bob Larsen was talking to the skipper when Max got off the chopper. In his absence, Mike Cullen had been re-assigned to the S1 position at Regiment. A new second lieutenant was being indoctrinated on a major combat operation, much as Max had been on Mameluke Thrust when he first arrived.

Larsen brought Max up to date on the latest casualties from their OCS class. So far, of their class of forty-five infantry officers, sixteen were dead and many others were wounded. Dave Lampkin, who'd chosen amphibious tractors, or Amtracs, as his occupational specialty, hit his third landmine and was blown off the top of his trac and wounded for the third time. With three purple hearts, he was going home..

* * * * * *

The next few weeks consisted of mostly company-sized sweeps through villages and hamlets in the valley. One day the ARVN would set up as a blocking force and the Marines would sweep the VC into their laps. Other days, the Korean Marines, fearless fighters, would do the sweeping and the Marines from Third Battalion, including K Company, would do the blocking.

The enemy resistance was not great, but casualties occurred almost daily. Three Marines and two navy corpsman died one day when a young stocky corpsman, HM Richardson, was wounded and another corpsman and four Marines went to his aid. As they carried him to the medevac chopper one of the Marines tripped another SFD, killing all but one Marine—and he lost both legs.

The First Platoon was pinned down in a rice paddy one day by heavy rifle and automatic weapons fire from the village they were approaching. Max called for air support and ordered "nape and snake", alternating runs of napalm and two hundred fifty pound bombs.

The sortie of two Marine F4B Phantoms out of Danang came in low but none too soon. The black, orange and yellow fireball spread across the village in an instant before billowing skyward. The second wave of death and destruction followed with the deafening thunder of the bombs. Each jet made two runs and was then gone almost as quickly as it had arrived.

"Kilo One, this is Bluebird, that should ruin Charlie's day," the lead pilot radioed, almost cheerfully. "Are you in need of any further assistance?"

Max took the handset from Corporal Shane. "Negative Bluebird. That was good shooting. We thank you, over."

"Roger then Kilo One, we're going home for lunch. This is Bluebird out." The pilots never got to see the corpses they left in their wake. Perhaps that explained their jolly attitude.

As the roar of the jets faded in the eastern sky, Max ordered the platoon to move out towards the village ahead. The enemy fire had ceased as the village with all its hooches and bamboo and banana trees burned and crackled, spewing ashes skyward. The figures of two persons silhouetted against the dancing flames walked from the inferno towards the platoon. They did not appear to be carrying weapons.

"Hold your fire!" Max shouted. The boy was approximately ten years old. He was barefoot and wore baggy shorts. Only scorched, tattered remains of what was a shirt stuck to the burned flesh that covered most of his upper torso. The boy walked in shock, staring straight ahead as the old man, not quite so badly burned, held his hand. They walked past Max and kept going, the offensive stench of seared flesh filling his nostrils, and close enough to the boy as he passed to see body fluids seeping through the red and black third degree burns. Their passing taunted him as if they were saying, "you did this." Max didn't know it then but that image would be a source of nightmares for many years after the war.

The Marines watched from the edge of the rice paddy as the village burned to the ground. Not much remained in the ashes but burned remnants of pottery and other household items, along with a water buffalo whose body still smoldered, and the charred corpses whose remains were indistinguishable as to gender or age.

The following day as the platoon prepared to move out, Max ordered PFC Corbett, whose broken ankle had since healed, to saddle up and join his squad on patrol. Corbett protested, asserting his ankle still hurt and he couldn't go on patrol. Max gave him a direct order to move out. He didn't fully hear what Corbett mumbled behind his back other than several expletives.

Private Dawson was still his usual pain in the ass. He and Corbett made a great pair. They were each other's best buddies and had no others, as the rest of the platoon knew they couldn't be counted on in a fire-fight when the chips were down. While Corbett was a big crybaby, Dawson was cunning. His haughty glance was never direct.

The memorial service following operation Taylor Common took place at Battalion. It was now February 1969. In Kilo Company alone, eleven men died and fifty-six were wounded. Scores of other Marines and allied forces also suffered heavy losses. If it offered any consolation, the enemy suffered heavy losses as well, many more than the allied forces, but they would keep coming and keep fighting.

Eleven M-16 rifles, bayonets affixed, were stuck into the ground, each supporting a helmet with the name of the dead Marine written across the camouflage cover. A pair of combat boots rested in front of each rifle and helmet. Captain Mitchell was called to a meeting with the battalion commander for a debriefing and told Max to stand before the company in his absence. Max choked up and fought back the tears as the bugler played taps.

After two days of rest in the Battalion CP, Max was called to the operations bunker to be briefed by the S-3, a major, on his next assignment. The VC were trying to blow up Nam-O Bridge, an eleven-hundred-foot steel bridge that spanned the inlet off the South China Sea north of Danang.

Highway 1, the only road out of Danang going north across Hai Van pass to Phu Bai and other points north, traversed Nam-O bridge. If the bridge was blown or captured, convoys would not be able to travel north from Danang, which would cut off all resupply except by air. The First Platoon was being sent to the bridge to hold it and prevent its destruction.

The S-3 drilled Max on the critical importance of not letting Nam-O fall to the enemy or be blown up. He told Max that if the bridge went, *he* went, meaning he would be re-assigned to a quite less-desirable job and location than he currently enjoyed. Likewise, if he went, then Lt. Max Elliot would also go, meaning that the S-3 would do all he could to see that Max got re-assigned to some other place.

In Max's case, however, that wasn't much of a threat. He'd already been in some of the worst places, had run harrowing missions and been in many firefights with the enemy. So just where could the major send him if he failed to defend the bridge? *Once you've been to hell, it all looks the same.* As one of his men had written on his helmet liner, "When I die, I'm going to heaven-I've spent my time in hell."

"You can have anything you want, just name it," the S-3 said, "but don't, and I repeat Lieutenant, *don't* lose that bridge!" The major had made his point.

Three six-bys transported the platoon to Nam-O Bridge to relieve the ARVN's who had held it thus far, but barely. A huge two-story French-built concrete bunker the size of a house was at the south end of the bridge. While eleven-hundred-feet long, the steel bridge was narrow, and the wooden deck was only a single lane wide. Max sized up the situation and decided what he would need to prepare his defense. He took the major up on his offer.

Max's shopping list consisted of two tanks, an 81mm mortar squad, engineers to plant a minefield, a mechanical mule with a 106 recoilless rifle mounted upon it, a 50 caliber machine-gun and cases of TNT along with electric blasting caps. Within hours, he had it all.

He set the mortars on the north end of the bridge that was open to the rice paddies leading to the mountains. He also set the 106 there with a quantity of flashette rounds capable of massive destruction against troops in the open that may attack from the north or northwest.

He ordered the 50 caliber machine-gun mounted on the roof of the bunker and could shoot in any direction, wherever needed. The two tanks remained on the east side of the bunker. One of the tanks came with the added benefit of a large xenon spotlight, mounted so that it moved with the turret and the 90mm canon.

The engineers went quickly to work planting a minefield and setting up concertina wire between the bunker and the beach that lay to the east. Max felt vulnerable from an attack through the village just to his south and along the beach.

Lastly, he ordered a roving patrol on the bridge itself. The squads would rotate in shifts, each shift spread out along the length of the bridge. The purpose of the bridge patrols was to watch the water more than anything else. Underwater VC sappers had been known to attach explosives to bridge supports and detonate them from a remote position. Max gave orders for his men to shoot at anything they saw floating in the river, but to keep their M-16's on semi-automatic. An automatic burst was the signal that sapper swimmers were confirmed in the area.

Additionally, each stick of TNT was cut into quarters and an electric blasting cap was placed in one end. The piece of explosive was then lowered into the water by the wire and the two wires were then touched to a PRC 25 radio battery taped to the bridge railing. The resultant underwater explosions, set off at two bridge locations every ten minutes during daylight hours and every five minutes during the night may not have killed any VC but drastically reduced the fish population.

The first night passed uneventfully, but a fifty percent alert was established and the platoon along with its attachments was ready for Charlie. The second day was quiet as well, except that the tank commander for the section decided he would take his tank on a little cruise through the village just to the south of the bridge, as sort of an intimidation run. As he passed a Vietnamese man on a bicycle, the cyclist most likely became unnerved by the passing of the 50 ton vehicle, lost control of his bike and fell into the road wheels of the tank.

As his body levigated between the wheels and the track, what oozed out from behind the rear wheels looked much like ground beef. The tank platoon commander, Lt. Cahan, had remained with his heavy section, but was summoned to Nam-O Bridge to conduct an investigation. There was little to investigate and in the end, the poor Vietnamese man was still very much macerated.

During the very early hours of the third day, at about 0100, incoming mortar rounds wounded one of the Marines from the mortar section at the north end of the bridge. The bridge took a few direct hits, but other than some splintered boards, the structural steel was unaffected by the mortars. The fourth day and night passed with little activity.

On the fifth day, Max was talking to Sgt. Gorman as they walked the length of the bridge, across and back. "Look at that sky Sarge," Max said.

"It's clouding up pretty good, Lieutenant. It's gonna be a dark night tonight."

"I have a feeling Charlie will be coming to pay us a visit. We better be alert."

"Right, Lieutenant, I'll see that everyone's on their toes tonight."

As they crossed the midpoint of the bridge on their way back to the command bunker, Max said to Sgt. Gorman, "You know Sarge, somehow I can't help feeling like Alex Guinness on the bridge over the River Kwai."

"I just hope this bridge doesn't end up the same way that one did," Gorman answered.

"Yeah, that makes two of us," Max replied.

Sure enough, at 2300 hours that dark, moonless night, the Viet Cong attacked from the beach to the east of the bunker on the south end of the bridge. The first warning of the attack came when the VC, attempting to breach the concertina wire entered the minefield and started blowing themselves up. As their agonizing screams bellowed in the night, the tank with the xenon light scanned the beach illuminating scores of enemy running every which way. Max ordered the mortar section to pepper the beach while concurrently sending up flares to illuminate the action. The 50 caliber machine-gun on the roof of the bunker was put into action and the tracers made for a light show. The tankers let loose with their canons and in the end Charlie lost, big time. No friendly casualties were incurred and VC bodies littered the beach.

The next day the major drove out to congratulate Max on the good job he was doing. He also advised him that he had been promoted to First Lieutenant and when Max returned to Battalion, the Colonel would officially promote him.

Max really didn't care much about the accolades because in reality, the major was more concerned about his own ass should Kilo One lose control of the bridge or the bridge became heavily damaged. What Max really wanted was for the major to leave so he could read the mail that he'd brought along, most particularly, another letter from Amber.

She had quit working the streets at Max's direction and found a part-time job as a salesclerk in a card and gift shop. Her letters were warm and well written. She always expressed her concern for Max's well being and then would write about all the things they would do when he came back to Sydney. Amber had also contacted her family and while not ready to return home, at least had reopened a line of communication. She expressed her love for Max in the letter, and it was that love, coupled with the love he felt in return, that made him feel somewhat human again for the moment.

Amber wrote regularly, sometimes sending letters several days in a row. Max read and re-read every letter many times over. They were his lifeline to sanity. One day he planned to be done with the war and then he and Amber would settle down. He'd be a good father to Amy. He dreamed of getting back to Australia in the worst way, yet while he had to defend Nam-O Bridge, that would be impossible.

It was two weeks before his relief came. When Kilo One got back to Battalion, he put in for a second R&R. He was turned down. The Battalion operations officer had another job for the First Platoon.

Max was beginning to feel like he commanded a bastard platoon, now separated from his company for almost three weeks. Pete Mitchell wasn't pleased to be minus one of his platoons either, but he was outranked and had little say in the matter. The First Platoon was assigned to ride security on the convoys transiting from Danang over the Hai Van Pass to Phu Bai, ironically also going across Nam-O Bridge. If the convoy got hit, First Platoon was to disembark the six-bys and engage the enemy.

That night, however, Max was once again summoned to the command bunker. "What's up now, Major?" he asked.

"A platoon from Mike Company is in heavy contact with the enemy and fear they may be about to be overrun. Get your platoon saddled and ready to lift off the LZ to assist. The choppers are coming to pick you up ASAP."

"Yes Sir," Max said. What else could he say? Orders were orders and not meant to be disobeyed. As he exited the bunker, the monsoon rains came. The night was dark—very dark—and now with the heavy rains, visibility was nil. He wondered how the choppers could navigate in such conditions. He wasn't about to disembark in the night and not know his precise coordinates.

As ordered, he got his men ready and they sat along the edge of the LZ in the downpour, soaking wet and shivering in the cold. They waited, and waited, and waited. After two and a half hours of shivering in the rain, the rescue mission was called off. The Mike Company platoon had not been overrun after all and the helicopters wouldn't fly in the poor visibility. It was a welcomed relief to spend the rest of the night out of the rain.

The next day Kilo One was aboard three six-bys in Danang, prepared to make a trip of forty-six miles over the pass to Phu Bai. While the convoy assembled, about half a dozen Vietnamese whores stood in the tree line soliciting the waiting Marines.

While none of the Kilo One Marines were allowed, a number of other young troops from the motor transport battalion entered and left the tree line, having consummated their acts in the woods. Returning to the trucks, they were minus a few piasters but smiling in spite of the fact that they had probably just paid for a good dose of the clap.

There were one-hundred and seventeen vehicles in the convoy that stretched for miles. Max put himself and the second squad on a truck in about the middle of the convoy. The first squad was on another vehicle near the front of the convoy and the third squad was on a third six-by near the rear. Movement up the mountain pass was slow. The convoy moved at a snail's pace of perhaps fifteen or twenty miles per hour at best.

Max learned at the start of the convoy run that the lieutenant who'd commanded the last platoon to ride shotgun was shot in his chest as he stood in the bed of the truck. His name was Randall Wilson—another OCS classmate. In Quantico, Randy was called "Pops," because a severe case of teenage acne had left his face scarred and looking like an old man's. Pops had been a friend but now he too was among Max's dead Quantico classmates.

Once over the top, the convoy accelerated rapidly on the way down. There were reports of some sniper fire, but nothing significant enough to get Kilo One off the trucks and in pursuit. At the bottom of the pass was a long straight run of eleven-hundred meters that was known as "the bowling alley." It was here that Charlie had his mortars registered.

As slow as the convoy ascended the mountain pass, it was the opposite on the downhill run towards the bowling alley. Max was not sure how fast a six-by could go but was certain the vehicles were running flat out. The mortar rounds came but the only casualty was a *water-buffalo*, not the four-legged kind, but the two-wheeled tankers towed behind a truck to carry water. It had been peppered with shrapnel and now leaked like water passing through a piece of Swiss cheese. And, one tire was shredded.

On the return trip, the First Platoon had to disembark and chase some elusive enemy who were shooting at the trucks during the slow climb up the north-slope pass.

Kilo One made four round trips over a two-week period and was glad to be off that job and back with the company. Pete Mitchell was equally ecstatic to have his platoon back. The First Platoon joined the Second and Third Platoons as the company went on a combat patrol. The patrol was only to last two days but ended up lasting five.

There was occasional contact with VC and always booby traps—but what made it almost unbearable were the monsoon rains. When wet, the men shivered and froze. Bill Cranston, the new second lieutenant in command of the Third Platoon, was killed during a firefight when he took an AK-47 round through his left temple. Thankfully, he never knew what hit him. Max had gotten to like the cocky Harvard grad who died in the mud. A poncho covered his body until the sky cleared enough to get a chopper in to pick up the wounded and the late lieutenant.

That night, Corporal Shane told Max about how the men in the platoon liked him and respected his leadership, with the possible exception of Pvt. Dawson and PFC. Corbett. It was raining again off and on in droves.

Max was terribly fatigued after more than nine months in combat with only that one week of R&R in Australia. *Yes, that one wonderful week.*

And then, for the first time in all his months in Vietnam, Max Elliot, huddled alone in a foxhole and cried. Whether it was the death that day of Bill Cranston, the physical and mental exhaustion of relentless duty, or just missing a certain girl in Australia, he didn't know and didn't care.

He let his tears run and struggled to subdue the sounds of grief that accompany an emotional breakdown. He couldn't let Cpl. Shane or anyone else know that their leader was crouched in his foxhole, crying. He cried until there were no more tears and he felt spent.

He reflected on his life. He thought about how it didn't seem so long ago when he asked his dad for a few bucks to go see a movie. He reflected on high school and college, replaying those events that took place his senior year that led him to make the choice that eventually brought him here. The crying was cathartic, a much-needed release.

He regained his composure and felt in control of himself. He could control his men if need be. He also knew it was time to get back to Australia and to the young woman he so desperately missed.

When the company got back to the Battalion compound a few days later, Max took a jeep and drove over to Regiment. He immediately went to see his old friend, Mike Cullen.

"Max, good to see you!" Mike said.

"Good to see you too, Mike. Looks like you've gained a few pounds sitting on your ass in this cushy job you got."

"I tell you, it may be cushy, but all this pencil pushing is a real pain in the ass. Sometimes I really miss the bush."

"Yeah, I'll bet you really miss getting your ass shot at and eating C's," Max said.

"Say, how about some hot chow? We got a pretty decent mess hall here."

"Sounds great, but Mike, first I have to ask you for a really big favor."

"Sure, what is it?"

"I need another R&R right away," Max said.

"No big deal. I handle all the R&R quotas for the Regiment."

"I know that," Max said. "That's why I'm asking you."

"Where do you want to go? Penang, Hong Kong, Bangkok? I have an opening for Kuala Lumpur, how's that?"

"Sydney," Max said. "I want to go to Sydney."

"But you already went to Sydney and that's the most demanded R&R destination. I can't give you another R&R to Sydney!"

Max leaned across the desk and spoke softly but emphatically in a way that Mike could see the desperation in his eyes. "Mike, I must get to Sydney!"

"It's a girl, isn't it?"

"Yes."

Mike Cullen looked at his friend with understanding. He hesitated, then told him, "You're out of here tomorrow."

"Thanks Mike. Thank you very much."

"Now," Mike said, "can we eat?

CHAPTER 12

Back Down Under

"Catch the ball, Amy! Good! Now roll it back to Mommy."

From the adjacent kitchen Oli called, "Dinner is on!"

Amber lifted Amy into her arms and hugged her. "We'll play some more later. Aunt Oli made us dinner."

They sat down and began to eat. "So, what did you tell him?" Oli asked.

"I said no, that's what I told him," Amber replied.

"But you don't know when that Marine is coming back. And I hate to say it, but you don't know *if* he's even coming back."

"Oli, don't ever say that again! You hear me?"

"Okay, okay. But that's the fifth GI to ask you out and you keep turning them down. I just want you to start having a good time, that's all."

"I'm doing just fine," Amber assured her. "I don't want to be with anyone else. Max will come back. I know he will. He said in his last letter that he had a friend who would help him get another R&R."

Oli looked at her and smiled. "You're really sweet on this guy, aren't you?"

"More than any man I have ever known."

"But you only knew him a few days before he left."

Amber smiled back at Oli. "And those were the most wonderful few days of my life."

"For the life of me, I'll never know what you two could write so much about. You must account for half of all the mail between Australia and Vietnam!"

"Yeah, and tell me you wouldn't like to have accounted for the other half?" Amber said.

"Me? Nah! I was never one for mushy romances. Men are strictly business." Yet, there was a quiver of uncertainty in her voice.

"Oli?"

"Yeah."

"Didn't you ever *really* love someone? A man, I mean?"

Oli hesitated, "Once I did." She paused. "His name was Robert... Robert Fadden. And was I in love...we were going to be married."

"Why didn't you?" Amber asked.

This time, the tears Amber suspected Oli was struggling with, won. A single tear fell upon her cheek. "Robert was an opal miner. He said we would be rich someday with him mining that way. But he died instead. His bloody damn mine killed him. Caved in and buried him alive. It was three days before they could even get his body out."

Amber reached out and touched Oli's forearm. "I'm really sorry," she said. "You never mentioned him before."

"What's there to mention? He's dead. And so, life has been a continuous downhill struggle ever since." Oli wiped away her tear, sniffled and continued to eat her dinner.

Just then the phone rang. "I'll get it," Amber said.

"No, you feed that hungry baby and let me get it. It's probably that Earle fella from the pub. Said he'd come over and fix this leaky tap today." Oli picked up the telephone. "Cheers," she said, then a short pause. "Yes, she is, one moment. Amber! If the devil himself ain't listening. It's him, honey."

Amber cupped her hands to her mouth. "Oh my God! Max? Is it Max?"

"Alive and well I presume, unless a ghost knows how to ring you up."

Amber shot from her chair and captured the phone from Oli. "Max, is it really you?"

"Were you expecting someone else?"

"Oh no, just you. Where are you?"

"Just checked into the Chevron. I wanted to make sure you were there. I'm coming right over."

"I can't believe you're here! You really *are* here!" Amber's enthusiasm was overwhelming. "No, don't come here. I'll come to you. Be there right away."

"Room 321."

"Bye."

* * * * * *

It was a long twenty minutes before the knock on the door. Max opened it and Amber stood there looking even more beautiful than he remembered, now radiating a more natural wholesome beauty with a look of a bit of tom-boyish and playful-mischief. The change in occupations obviously agreed with her—he saw no hardness in her lovely face.

For a long moment they just stared at each other, then Amber took a step forward and into his arms. Immediately, he was captivated by the smell of her hair and body which he longed for and could only dream about in Vietnam.

As he kissed her deeply, savoring the taste and feel of her against him, he ran his hand through her long, soft hair. He pulled her out of the doorway and into the room, closing the door behind them, and kissed her again.

"I've missed you," he said.

"Not more than I've missed you," she replied. "I *knew* you would come back. Has the war been hard on you?"

"It's getting real old," he said. "Men keep dying and for what? We keep killing the VC and NVA but nothing really changes. They keep coming. There are no victories in this war. We win battles and sometimes we lose a few, but always men die. Let's forget about the war, I'm here now."

"I prayed you wouldn't get hurt."

He smiled at her and nodded. "I'm glad you did. Thank you."

They didn't leave the room for several hours. Their love was powerful, yet gentle, and the void left by months of separation was amorously filled by two people from different worlds drawn to each other by fate or circumstance.

As they cuddled in an embrace, Max thought of all the crossroads in life, and how, at each such intersection, one must choose a road that either led to happiness or tragedy, success or failure, even life or death.

Had he not chosen to join the military, where would he be? Had he not met Amber, would he not have taken a second R&R and if so, would he have become a casualty of war instead?

And Amber, what choices brought her here? Had she not gotten involved with Gordon Hamilton would she have remained at her parent's station, the Sunrise? And what if she hadn't met Max on the streets of Kings Cross one day months ago, would her life had continued its downward trend devoid of any self-respect?

By fate or by chance, by the hand of the Almighty or by pure coincidence, Max knew there was absolutely nowhere else on the planet he would rather be than in Amber's arms. His love for a one-time prostitute was inexplicable.

"Max?" Amber murmured.

"What?"

"Would you take me home?"

"I've only been here a few hours and you're tired of me already?" he said with a soft laugh.

"No, I mean *really* home—to the Sunrise."

"Is this going to be a temporary visit or are you going to stay?" he asked.

"I'm not sure. Things are going fairly well lately. Mrs. Cochran, the lady who owns the shop I work at is really good to me, and Amy and I are able to make it on our own. So, I don't know."

"When do you want to go?"

"Tomorrow."

"Then tomorrow we'll go."

"Mother has never seen Amy. I wonder how she'll take to her?"

"Like a grandmother, that's how she'll be."

"I can't believe I'm going home."

"Well, start believing, but first we have to contend with each other for one long boring night," Max said facetiously.

"Oh yeah!" she said as she rolled on top of him, her firm breasts only inches from his face. "I'll show you how boring it will be."

* * * * * *

In the morning they had coffee at the hotel before collecting Amy from Oli. Then they headed for breakfast.

"Come join us, Oli," Amber said.

"Sure, why don't you?" Max added.

"Nah, you kids go ahead. I've got more important things to do than listen to a couple of cackling lovebirds."

"Oli?"

"Now what? I thought you were going for breakfast."

"Max, Amy and I are going to the Sunrise."

Oli was stunned for a moment. She put her arm on Amber's shoulder.

"That's good. That is *really* good, Luv. Will you be staying?"

"No, maybe just for a few days. I don't think I could go back permanently yet. Besides, Amy and I aren't ready to leave you all by yourself, unless of course you're ready to throw us out."

"You're the best friend I've got, kid. And this one," she said as she placed her hand under Amy's chin, "I love like she were my very own, but I want what's best for you two, or three, whatever, and don't you be worrying about old Oli here." With that she handed Amber her keys. "Take the jeep, I can do without it a few days."

Amber hugged Oli. "Thanks. You're my best friend, too."

The three-hundred and seventy mile trip took eight hours in the old jeep. Amber got more and more anxious the closer they got.

"Stop here, Max."

He pulled the jeep off to the side of the road. "Why are we stopping?" he asked.

"I'm scared, Max."

"Of what?"

"What if they hate me?"

"Don't be ridiculous. Why would they hate you?"

"It was probably my fault that father died."

"That's not true and don't ever think that again."

"I'll always feel somewhat responsible for father's death...I must have broken his heart." She sniffed and put on a brave smile. "Well, we've come this far, let's go. The gate into the Sunrise is just around the next bend."

Two wagon wheels were propped against the poles that supported the overhead wooden sign into which was carved "Sunrise." Max steered the jeep off the paved road and started down the long dusty drive.

"Well, we're here," she said with a nervous sigh as Max turned off the ignition.

Delia McEwen heard the jeep pull up and stood on the porch as they approached. Her face turned ashen and no words came from her lips as Amber now stood before her with Amy in her arms. The two looked at each other, each afraid to speak first.

Amber broke the silence. "Mother, this is your granddaughter, Amy." Delia put her hand on Amy's head and softly stroked the child's hair. The baby looked at the woman as if sensing a kindness and belonging. Delia then focused on Amber and began to cry. Amber embraced her mother as Delia put her arms around both of them.

"Oh mother, I've missed you so much," her voice quivered and her eyes filled with joyous tears.

Max felt a lump in his throat. Amber stepped away from her mother and turned to face Max.

"Mother, this is Max Elliot. Max, my mother."

"You may call me Delia."

"It's my pleasure," he said.

Delia now placed her hands on Amber's shoulders. "Let me look at you," she said smiling. "You're a little skinny, but otherwise you look pretty much the same."

"Mother, Max is from America. He's a Marine lieutenant serving in Vietnam."

"Well, come on in and tell me all about it. You must be starved. I'll start dinner."

"Let me help you," Amber insisted. "Max, would you mind occupying Amy for awhile?"

"Not at all," he said as he took her from Amber.

In the kitchen, Delia asked, "You haven't seen your brother yet, have you?"

"No, we came straight to the house. Is John all right?"

"Oh yes, he's quite well. He and some of the stockman are rounding up some brumbies they intend to break. He should be here shortly."

Max was playing with Amy on the couch when John came in. "You must be John?"

"I am," he replied, obviously puzzled by the presence of a strange man and child in his home.

Max smiled and gently tugged Amy to his side. "I'm Max Elliot. This is Amy, your niece."

"My niece? You mean to tell me Amber is here?"

Just then, having heard John's voice, Amber appeared from the kitchen. She ran into open arms that wrapped around her as he whirled her around. "I can't believe it!" he said. "You're really home! How are you?"

"I'm good...really good. You've met Max?"

"Yes, we've already met."

They sat down for dinner. Indulging more than the others, Max eagerly feasted on the roast lamb, boiled potatoes and fresh garden vegetables. As they ate, Amy was the center of attention. "How old is she?" John asked.

"She'll be fifteen months next week," Amber proudly answered.

"If she isn't the prettiest little thing you ever laid eyes on," John professed.

"She looks just like you did at that age, Amber," Delia stated.

"You going to let Uncle John teach her to ride, Sis?"

Amber laughed. "Not quite so soon, but perhaps when the time comes."

"Well, we got to get her started sometime. We have some buckjumpers need taming or are you gonna be around to help out?"

There was a moment of silence at the table. "I don't think so, John. I have a job in Sydney. I have to go back."

"Oh, I'm sorry to hear that," John acknowledged, obviously disappointed. "And what about you, Max? Tell me about America?"

"Well, what do you want to know?"

"You're a Marine I'm told."

"That's right."

"Tough job you boys got over there in Vietnam, isn't it?"

Max really did not want to talk about Vietnam, but also didn't want to be impolite either. "Yes, it is a tough job… kind of a thankless one too. I've worked with some Australian troops there. Good fighting men."

"Yeah, long as they get their ale, they'll fight. Australia has lost many men over there you know, but not nearly as many as America has lost."

Amber sensed Max's uneasiness. "Max can ride, John. We rode outside Sydney last December. In the mountains."

"Oh, so you've known each other a while then?" Delia asked.

"Yes Mother, since December, on Max's first R&R."

"Amber, I hate to bring this up, but Hamilton was here about a week ago looking for you," John said.

"What did you tell him?" she asked with a degree of panic.

"The truth. I didn't know where you were. He didn't believe me, but I wouldn't have told him if I did know."

"What happened?" she asked.

"I asked him where you were. He said you left him. Then I ran him off."

"Good. I hope I never see the likes of him again," she asserted.

Following dinner they all sat on the veranda and talked for hours. Delia and John regaled Max with Amber's escapades as a child on the Sunrise. Amber avoided, as best she could, all questions posed about her initial struggle in Sydney and particularly about her brief enrollment in prostitution. She did, however, tell her family about Gordon Hamilton's abuse.

"That doesn't surprise me," John stated. "After you left, folks started telling me things about him. When I finally was prepared to tell you, I called and some bloke named Hawker told me you took off; said he didn't know where you went but couldn't blame you for leaving. He also said Hamilton beat him up pretty bad for letting you get away. He's a mean one, that Hamilton."

Amber did not want any more reminders of her time with Gordon Hamilton. "I want to see Tuffy," she said. "Mother, would you mind Amy while Max and I go to the barn?"

"You go on, it's about time I get better acquainted with my granddaughter."

In comfortable silence, Amber took Max's hand and they strolled the long way to the barn.

"I sure missed the smell of this old place," Amber said as they walked into the large old wooden structure. "Here's Tuffy. Tuff old boy, how I missed you," she said as she stroked the bay's head and then kissed his muzzle. The gelding snorted and nuzzled his head closer to hers. There was no doubt that the gelding remembered his master.

Max patted Tuffy's neck. "He sure is a nice-looking horse."

"Father gave him to me when I was ten. Tuffy was only a yearling colt then. I broke him myself." Suddenly, Amber seemed despondent.

"What is it?" Max asked. "You look so sad."

"It's father. It seems so strange to be here and he's not here anymore. I wish you could have met him. You two would have gotten along fine. Father would have liked you."

Max put his arms around her from behind and kissed her neck. "I'm sure I would have liked him. I really like your mother and John."

Amber turned in Max's arms and looked into his eyes. "Max?"

"What?"

"Don't ever leave me."

Max looked back into the deep green eyes of the girl he so passionately loved. "I'll never leave you."

"I love you, Max."

"I love you, too." And in the dim light of the barn, they embraced.

"We can't sleep together tonight," she said.

"I know that. It's going to be a long, lonely night."

"Tomorrow we'll go riding. I know a place we can go and be alone."

"Sounds good to me. Why don't we go back up to the house now?"

"Okay," she said as she kissed him again.

The next day after a hearty breakfast of steak, eggs, potatoes and roasted tomatoes, Amber and Max rode out for the countryside, Amber astride Tuffy and Max on one of the station's other stock horses.

"This is really beautiful country," he said, inhaling the clear dry air.

"It is, isn't it?" she whispered.

There was an old wooden line-shack along the fringe of the station. They unsaddled their mounts and turned them loose in the corral. The shack was near a cliff whose precipice overlooked the fertile valley and river below.

"We winter the cattle down there," Amber pointed out as they savored the view.

"I see why you love it here. I could spend the rest of my life with you, right here," Max said.

"Don't you think the house is a little small?" Amber joked as she looked towards the deteriorating shack.

"Oh, I don't know. Let's go in and find out?"

The door creaked as they opened it. The shack consisted of a single room. In one corner was a kitchen, of sorts, which contained an old wood-burning stove, some shelves made of wooden crates nailed to the wall, and a table with two chairs, one with only three legs, the forth corner supported by a wooden box. In another corner was a bunk bed, upon each set of springs rested a thin mattress.

Other than a few buckets, an old unserviceable stock saddle with cracked and rotted leather parts, and a small woodpile near the stove, there was nothing else in the shack other than a small assortment of miscellaneous non-matching dishes, kitchen utensils and partially rusted skillets along with the few insects that scooted up the walls

"This will do just fine," Max said. "But of course we'll have to add another bedroom for the kids."

"Kids?" she questioned.

"Sure, you don't want Amy to grow up without any brothers and sisters do you?"

"No, I guess not."

"Well then, let's get in some more practice so when the time comes we'll have it down just right," Max said with a mischievous grin.

"No, I think I'll just save myself now for when that time comes," she said, hardly able to contain herself from laughing out loud.

"Bullshit!" Max blurted as he grabbed her and wrestled her to the lower of the two bunks.

"Stop that, you horny yank!" she said laughing. "I'm a respectable woman!"

Serious now, Max stopped. "You are a respectable woman, and you're my woman. I'm not sharing you with anyone."

Amber put her hand on the back of Max's neck. "Nor am I sharing you. If I ever catch you with another woman, I'll take a bullwhip to you."

"Well that does it then. I'm frightened to death. Guess I'll leave all those pretty little Vietnamese girls alone from now on."

"You better, or you'll answer to General McEwen here, buddy!"

"Now then General, will you shut up?" And he pressed his lips to hers. As the horses grazed and the warm winds blew through the open window of the line-shack his thoughts of the war so many thousand miles away and her thoughts of an abusive Gordon Hamilton were out of mind as they thought only of the love they felt together.

They walked the horses on the way back, enjoying the sunshine, the warm breezes, the scenery and each other. Near the barn Amber reined in Tuffy. "Oh my god!" she exclaimed.

"What is it?" Max asked, sensing her fear.

"It's him. Gordon is here! What'll I do?"

"Don't worry about him," Max said. "You don't have to run from him anymore. Let's go put the horses up and see what he wants."

John was already telling Hamilton to leave as they dismounted. "What do you want Gordon?" she asked sternly.

"Now don't be in a huff, deary," he said. I just came to see my child, that's all."

"Don't call me 'deary' you bloody bastard!"

"I see I didn't teach you enough respect," Gordon said.

"You better be going," Max said in his American drawl. "You've done all the teaching you're going to do."

"Well, well. So you've taken up with a yank, have you? How cozy."

"I said leave, Hamilton. And I mean now," Max asserted.

Gordon smirked while looking in Amber's direction. "Looks like I may have to teach your friend here a little bit about Australian manners."

Amber was frightened. "You leave him alone!" she exclaimed.

John intervened. "He's mine. I aim to finish what I should have finished once before. Hamilton, you're lower than sheep shit."

"I don't want to hurt you, John. We use to be drinking buddies, but if you insist..."

Max dropped the reins he held in one hand and grabbed Hamilton by his arm. "This is my last friendly warning for you to leave."

"Unhand me, Yank," Gordon said as he looked down at Max's firm grip on his bicep.

Max let loose his grip, but as he bent over to pick up the bridle reins, Gordon struck him with a quick right uppercut. Max fell back but was still on his feet. His lip was cut and he could already taste his blood in his mouth. Momentarily stunned by the unexpected blow, his head cleared quickly. He hadn't anticipated being a combatant in Australia. He thought he'd left that behind in Nam. A sudden rage surged within him and with the same fury he felt in a hostile firefight with the Viet Cong, he went after Gordon Hamilton.

Max was left-handed and Hamilton was taken by surprise with the left hook. Max didn't hesitate with that—he went for the kill. Two blows to Hamilton's abdomen buckled him over. Max then struck him on the back of his neck and he went down. Gordon propped himself up, coughed while holding his stomach with one hand, but got to his feet.

Max wrongly assumed Hamilton was down for the count. Gordon threw another punch that caught Max by surprise sending him back against the barn door. Hamilton closed in, but instead of punching Max, he kicked him in the groin.

The kick hurt, but not nearly as much as it would have if it had been an accurate shot. "So you want to play dirty, do you?" Max growled as he came out swinging. Some of his punches connected while likewise some of Hamilton's volleys sent in return also connected. But Max inflicted the heaviest damage. When one of Max's blows stood Hamilton upright, Max let him have it with a punch above his eye that opened it up, spewing blood down his face.

"That's enough!" Amber screamed.

John jumped between them and the two men stopped fighting. Both were breathing heavily. Hamilton bled from his mouth, but more profusely from the cut above his right eye. A trickle of blood also ran from Max's mouth where Hamilton's first uppercut drove the inside of his lip into his lower teeth.

"Now get the hell out of here, and if you ever bother her again, I'll kill you!" Max said, and meant it.

Hamilton said nothing. He glared at Max, John and then Amber, picked up his hat and staggered off to his truck.

"I think we've seen the last of him," John said.

"I hope so," said Amber.

"Pretty good fighting there, Marine," John said to Max.

Max touched his hand to his cut mouth. "Yeah, I can't wait to get back to Nam for some peace and quiet."

"Let me see that cut," Amber said.

"I'll be okay," Max said. "Let's put the horses up."

"You two go up to the house and put some ice on that lip. I'll see to the horses," John said.

Delia had watched the fight from the porch. "Are you all right, Max?" she asked.

"Yes ma'am, I'm okay, thank you," he said.

As they entered the house, Max started feeling pain in the inside of his right thigh where he had been kicked. "I'm sure glad he missed with that kick to my groin," he said to Amber out of earshot of Delia.

"So am I," she said with a smile that was unmistakable.

After lunch they took a walk, played with Amy, and cherished their time together. Max wished not only that he didn't have to return to Vietnam and the war, but that he could stay in Australia on the Sunrise with Amber and Amy, forever. He felt at peace with himself for the first time in many years. He felt a sense of belonging and while he was always too restless to settle down, that was not the case now. He loved it on the Sunrise. More importantly though, he loved Amber McEwen.

"I think we'll go back to Sydney tomorrow," she said.

"Are you sure? I don't mind staying here. In fact, this is great. I love it here," he said.

"I'm glad you like it. Maybe someday we'll be back."

"Let's plan on it," Max said.

"I wish you didn't have to go back to Vietnam."

Max wasn't quite sure what to say. He didn't want to go back either. He wished he could stay right where he was, but he knew that was impossible. He had an obligation with the Marine Corps that had to be fulfilled and he had an obligation to the men of the First Platoon—they depended on him.

"Amber?" he said as he put his arms around her.

"What?"

"When I get back to Nam, I have four more months to go, then I have to return to the States to finish my three year obligation with the Corps. I don't want us to be apart that long. I'll send for you. I want you and Amy to come to the States when I get back."

"I'll, I mean *we*, will go anywhere to be with you. I just worry so much that something awful will happen to you in Vietnam."

"I've made it this far, I'll make it to the end. Besides, I now have too much to live for."

They got a later start the next day than they intended, but finally they were on their way. "Mother really likes you," she said. "She thinks you're a fine young man."

"Is that what she said?" Max questioned.

"Sure did. Also thinks your accent is cute."

"I don't have an accent. It's you Aussies that talk funny."

Back in Sydney they spent their remaining days together, each day bringing them closer and closer. Each felt it was their destiny that they had been brought together, like some great order to the universe had preplanned all their life's experiences to lead up to their eventual union. They were comfortable with each other in all respects. And whatever magnetism created that initial infatuation, Max knew unconditionally that he was in love. Amber, likewise, had the man she wanted.

One afternoon when Mrs. Cochran needed Amber at the store and couldn't let her off, Max stayed at the flat with Amy. She was a really good child and rarely fussed unless some of her basic needs weren't met. He knew that he loved Amy, too. Like her mother, she was gorgeous, and while his experience with babies was limited, he did well with Amy and truly enjoyed caring for her in her mother's absence.

The day of departure came too soon. It was much more difficult to say goodbye this time than after his first R&R. Max dressed in his Marine uniform which commenced the transition from the sane world to that of the insane. The mere wearing of the uniform, complete with rank insignia, campaign ribbons and shooting badges, was a startling self-reminder of who he really was—an officer in the United States Marine Corps.

Before boarding the bus that would take him and the other Vietnam-bound warriors to the airport, Max lifted Amber's chin only to see tears in her eyes. He kissed her and held her tight.

He smelled her hair and touched it. He wanted to hold that feeling in his mind and to savor her scent until they would be together again.

CHAPTER 13

Wherever You Are, Be There

There is a saying: "wherever you are, be there" but Max struggled mightily with getting his head and heart which were in Australia with Amber and Amy, back to Vietnam where his body—and duty were. He knew how dangerous being distracted could be—for himself and the men he commanded.

The first month or so back was fairly routine. Combat patrols by day, ambushes by night. Occasionally the compound that the company or platoon happened to be in would come under attack, but they were never overrun.

One night a few sappers penetrated the Battalion perimeter but were killed before they detonated the charges strapped to their bodies. They'd been headed for the command bunker to blow it up along with themselves, much like the Japanese kamikaze pilots of WW II.

By spring, most of the original platoon had been replaced with new faces. Some of the original members of the First Platoon had been killed, more wounded, and the more fortunate completed their thirteen months and went "back to the world on the freedom bird."

Corporal Shane and Doc Shepherd were still around, but both were short timers. Sergeant Gorman rotated back to the States and Corporal Tanner, now Sergeant Tanner, was promoted by Max to Platoon Sergeant. Lance Corporal Pomeroy, since promoted to corporal, was now the squad leader of the Third Squad, replacing Corporal Garrison who had been killed.

Pomeroy occasionally received letters from PFC Ingersoll who had been wounded in the ambush near Thuong Duc last year. He was recovering well and received his honorable medical discharge from the Corps in March.

Unfortunately, Pvt. Dawson and PFC Corbett, both still at their prior ranks, were still around. Dawson, because of his brig time last year, had to make that time up so his tour was extended. Both remained the black sheep of the platoon.

There was a heavy monsoon rain the day the First Platoon was to relieve a platoon from L Company occupying a platoon patrol base, creatively referred to as a PPB. Kilo One would be there about "a week or two."

Three six-bys drove the First Platoon along the muddy road as close to the PPB as they could get, which happened to be within twelve-hundred meters. Max had the grid coordinates, AT973642, and proceeded to move his platoon towards their destination. The surrounding rice paddies were flooded in the monsoon rain. Most of the paddy dikes were also under water. Only some of the taller dikes that sparsely segmented the vast valley were above water but they were muddy.

So the Marines slogged along, moving from one muddy dike to the next, the only way they could cross the flooded terrain. The driving rain blew in sheets with such force that it ran almost parallel to the ground rather than perpendicular to it. Some men wore their ponchos over their flak jackets, packs and other gear, but except for providing a little warmth, those did little to keep them dry. One of the newer replacements, PFC Potts, a six-foot bespectacled troop, slipped on the muddy dike and into the paddy that had a water depth exceeding his stature. Weighted down with his gear, Potts plummeted beneath the surface. The two Marines nearest him lay down on the dike and fished him out. Potts never let go of his M-16, and other than being covered with mud and having swallowed some water, he fared well in his aquatic ordeal.

It was mid afternoon when the sodden troops reached the PPB. Home for the next week or so was a triangular shaped base about fifty yards on each of its three sides, which was constructed during the dry season and consisted of nothing more than a dirt parapet about ten feet high bulldozed into place. Within its perimeter were two GP medium military tents, each now flooded with six inches of water, as was the rest of the base. The troops either sat on the inside of the berm or on ammo cases, or whatever else kept their feet out of the water.

Max immediately recognized First Lieutenant Phil Renfro, one of his OCS classmates, as he entered the tent. "So this is where you been hiding all these months."

"Well, the past three weeks anyway. How are you, Max?"

"I'm doing okay Phil, how about you?"

"Just marking time and trying to stay alive another two months," Phil said.

"Yeah, I guess we're becoming short timers."

"You know, there's not many of us from Quantico left."

"Yeah, sad isn't it?"

Phil nodded. "So what the hell have you been doing all year?"

"Well, I was up north with the Ninth for awhile. When they came south I was transferred to the First as S3 Alpha for five months, then given this platoon with Lima Company."

"How long have you been skating out here?" Max asked.

"Like I said, three weeks. Wasn't too bad until a few days ago when the rains wouldn't let up. Most of us don't have much skin left on our feet anymore."

"Charlie been visiting any?" Max asked.

"Oh yeah, he's been real neighbor-like. Likes to sneak up at night mostly. I've been in worse places and I'm sure you have too, but don't let your guard down. I think Charlie is planning to overrun this hole and up to this point has just been testing us."

"Thanks for the info. You moving out tonight?" Max asked.

"Nah, it's getting too late. We'll pull out in the morning."

"Good," Max said. "Why don't we split the perimeter tonight and get settled in?"

"Sounds good to me," Phil said.

The officers directed their respective platoon sergeants to set up the appropriate security and watches for the remainder of the day and night. The rain continued in torrents, and some of the men in first platoon made little lean-tos with empty ammo crates, C-ration boxes, sticks and whatever else they could find to support their ponchos which comprised the roofs of their makeshift shelters.

"Why don't we sit in my office for awhile," Phil said jokingly. Inside the tent he had several crates of 60mm mortar rounds piled to create a place to sit and keep his feet dry.

"Cigar?" Max offered. Max always carried cigars with him in Nam. Mostly Rum Crooks, those inexpensive sweet cigars he stocked up on at the PX. His distaste for c-rations grew more acute the longer he ate them, and often times he would just chew on a cigar, sometimes not even lit, as a pacifier to forego eating.

"Sure, I'll have a smoke," Phil said. "I'm out of cigarettes and those c-rat smokes are stale as hell."

"I don't smoke cigarettes," Max said. "Only smoke cigars to keep my mind off food. I usually eat more of these things than I smoke."

The night passed with no enemy activity. Max and Phil Renfro sat on the ammo crates and exchanged small talk most of the night. The rain continued but subsided some. About 0300 Max went to check his troops.

"Evenin' Lieutenant," said one of his men as Max passed by, sloshing through the mud and water.

"How you doing, Potts? Not thinking about going swimming again, are you?"

"Not tonight, Sir," PFC Potts answered. "I sure would like to dry off, though."

"Well, maybe we'll get lucky and we'll see the sun tomorrow," Max said.

"Hope so, Sir—I'm f-f-freezing."

Farther down the berm wall Max caught a whiff of the smoke. He was right next to Dawson and Corbett neither of whom had seen him coming in the darkness and rain. He stood there a moment before they saw him.

"Oh shit," Corbett said as he quickly extinguished the joint. Dawson cast a loathsome smirk, took another long drag and then proceeded to carefully put the joint out with his fingers.

"Smoking pot is a court martial offense, you know?" Max said.

In the eleven months he had been in Nam he had not had any incidents of any of his men smoking pot. For most of the Marine grunts in the bush who carried their possessions on their backs and depended on their alertness and that of their buddies to stay alive, pot wasn't near as much a problem.

Dawson said nothing. "You gonna have us court martialed Lieutenant?" Corbett asked with a tremor in his voice.

"I just might," Max said. "I'll let you know. But first, hand over all your pot."

"Lieutenant, Sir, this won't keep me from going on R&R next week, will it?"

"The *pot* Marine. Hand it over."

"Donnie's got it Sir. I don't have any," Corbett said in his whiney voice. He was shaking so bad at being caught Max thought he was probably peeing in his pants.

"Give it up, Dawson," Max insisted. Dawson glared back, with a look that in the darkness was still discernable as part-stoned and part-hatred. Then Dawson reached in his pocket and pulled out a Marlboro pack, picked out three joints from the pack and handed them over.

"All of them, Dawson," Max asserted.

"The rest of these are regular smokes," Dawson said.

"They better be," Max said as he moved on down the perimeter.

The next morning the rain let up to a drizzle, the sky remained dark grey and Lieutenant Renfro and his platoon prepared to leave. "I'm not humping any of this shit out of here Max. You've got cases of 5.56 and 7.62 link, and beaucoup grenades, H-E and willy-peter."

"See you around campus, Phil," Max said as the Lima Company platoon slogged away.

"Good luck," Phil replied as he turned and looked at Max before climbing over the slippery berm for the last time.

The departing platoon spread out in a line along the dikes as they moved off. In the distance they appeared to be walking on water, as only the very tops of the tallest dikes remained above the seasonal brown sea.

In the daylight Max surveyed the base. It was a mess. There was trash everywhere. Some ammo crates were full, others empty, but there was no time to take inventory, so the First Platoon went to work.

Just outside the berm on the north side, the dozers that built the base had dug a large pit about fifty feet out. It was large enough and deep enough that a large car could be buried in it. Its purpose was to use for trash and it was about one third full of it along with water.

The heavy rains had caused somewhat of a minor mud-slide on the berm walls and as the men prepared their own little positions along the perimeter they found scores of live grenades in the mud left behind by their predecessors. Sergeant Tanner began collecting them in a common area and had a pile collected that could fill a duffel bag.

Max's next order of business was to get his one 60mm mortar registered so when darkness fell and they came under attack his 60 mike-mike guys could get the rounds on target. There were no villages to the immediate east, the direction of the road where they came in.

Likewise, to the north and south there were no villages within eight hundred meters, but to the west, the village of Thai Cam rose like an island in the sea about three-hundred meters out.

Max's orders included strict rules of engagement and he was to request permission from the battalion operations officer before he could fire, unless of course he was fired upon first. Typical of the political restraints placed upon the military in what the news had dubbed a "police action." Max checked in.

"That's a negative, Kilo One," said the S3. "That's a friendly ville out there. Permission granted to register mortar to north, south and east, but not west. I say again, negative on registering sixty mike-mike to the west."

And so, in the highest, driest spot the mortar guys could find, they built their own little mortar pit, a circle about six feet in diameter with a foot high berm around it. Sticks stuck in the small parapet acted as aiming stakes, so in darkness they would move the handheld mortar to a particular stake and know in which direction the mortar round would go. Then all they had to do was raise or lower the tube to get the correct elevation and subsequent distance.

That night all hell broke loose. Every fifth round of link ammo for the M-60 machine-guns is a tracer round, a red phosphorus projectile that allowed the gunner to see where his bursts were going. The enemy also had tracer rounds but theirs were white rather than red.

The light show was maniacal. Red tracers streamed from the two M-60's and streams of white tracers came in from as many guns. Not surprising, the incoming small arms and machine-gun fire emanated from Thai Cam. As best they could, the mortar men lobbed rounds into the ville. Concurrently, Max called in a fire mission from the 105mm Howitzer battery in general support.

"Hotshot, this is Kilo One, right 100, add 50, fire for effect!" Max coolly directed over the radio as the artillery now fell on target. "Repeat!" he instructed as another volley was requested.

"They're hitting us on the north side, Lieutenant!" Sergeant Tanner screamed out from his position on the berm.

"Shit! Move that gun from the left corner to the middle of the berm!" Max commanded as the two machine-gunners quickly changed position. "Start tossing those grenades on all sides!"

"They're in the trash pit!" someone shouted. Several Marines on the north berm starting hurling grenades, one of which happened to be a white phosphorous, mixed in the pile left behind by Lima Company. The grenade detonated within the trash pit and lit the sky in brilliant white light while the unfortunate Viet Cong inside shrieked at the onset of his cremation. Another, having escaped the inferno met death by a shower of rifle and machine-gun fire as he exited the pit.

In twenty minutes it was all over. The trash pit continued smoldering the rest of the night, and the men stayed on one hundred percent alert. In the early morning mist the blackness turned to gray. Then, in an awesomely spectacular array of color the sun partially revealed itself in the eastern sky far beyond the flooded paddies, barely peeking above the horizon yet spewing its divided rays among the clouds in shades of amber.

Max felt good that morning. In symbolic beckoning, the "amber dawn" brought warm thoughts to an otherwise drenched and chilled body, of a love far away. He wondered if the late George McEwen eyed a similar sky in hues of yellowish brown on the morning of his daughter's birth, giving rise to her name—Amber Dawn.

After his men had a chance to heat coffee and some morning chow, Max led a patrol of two squads, Alpha and Bravo, leaving the third squad at the PPB. It was a short patrol into the village of Thai Cam so Max told his men to leave their packs behind. Thai Cam had been mostly destroyed following the artillery barrage from the night before. Nine VC bodies lay among the ruins. Most likely others had been carried away or escaped. Counting the two bodies by the trash pit, there were eleven enemy KIA confirmed. There were no indications of civilians. Kilo One had suffered no casualties.

While Corbett, a member of the second squad, was on the patrol, Dawson, who was in the third squad, remained in the PPB. He was snooping around when he saw the lieutenant's pack on the ammo crate. No one else was in the tent. Dawson opened the pack and went through Max's belongings. A poncho liner, extra socks, shaving gear, letter writing supplies, maps, grease pencils, a can of tuna fish, cigars, a paperback book- "Exodus" by Leon Uris, an extra pair of utility trousers, and five or six letters bound with an elastic band.

Dawson noticed that all the letters bore Australian postage. He looked at the return addresses. They were all the same- Miss Amber McEwen, 3701 Burra St., Sydney, New South Wales, Australia. Dawson pulled one of the letters from the center of the stack and slipped it into his pocket. He returned the rest to the pack, closed it back up to appear undisturbed and left the tent, careful to see that no one had seen him.

Later that day after the patrol had returned, Corbett was again with Dawson. "Do you think the lieutenant is going to have us court martialed Donnie?" Corbett asked.

"Fuck him. Let me show you what I got." Dawson then pulled the letter from his pocket. "The Lieutenant has got him a honey in Australia, some chick named 'Amber.' There's this other chick she lives with named 'Oli'."

"Where'd you get that"! Corbett exclaimed. "That's the Lieutenant's mail."

"Not anymore."

"What are you planning, Donnie?"

"You'll see."

* * * * * *

Checking her mailbox each day for a letter from *First Lieutenant Max Elliot, K Company, Third Battalion, First Marines, FMF WestPac,* was the highlight of her day. Often times she would sit on the front steps of the bungalow waiting for Mr. Travers, the postman, to arrive.

Mr. Travers knew what she was waiting for and he was happy for her when the appropriate postmark arrived. "We've got one today!" he said with exuberance.

"Thank you, Mr. Travers!" she said cheerfully. Amber sat back down on the front steps and opened the letter, perplexed by the return address in the upper left hand corner that wasn't Max's writing. Amy played on the grass nearby.

Dear Miss McEwen,

My name is Sergeant Jones and I serve in Vietnam with the 1st Marines. I am also in the same unit as Lt. Max Elliot who has spoken highly of you. I regret to inform you that Lt. Elliot was killed in action on May 23, 1969 by hostile enemy fire while on patrol in an area south of Danang, Vietnam.

I am sorry to have to be the one to bring you this bad news.

Sincerely,
Sgt. Robert Jones

The color drained from her face. "No!" she cried out. "No, God, tell me it's not true!" Amy sensed her mother's anguish and came to her side, supporting herself on her mother's leg. Amber picked Amy up into her arms and buried her head into the babies shoulder. She cried. She rocked back and forth holding Amy tightly, and cried more... then more.

* * * * * *

Four days later, while still at the patrol base, Max called Corbett into the tent. "Corbett, I just learned we are pulling out of here tomorrow. You are also scheduled to go on R&R in two days. I've been debating what to do with you."

"But Sir, I..." Max interrupted.

"Listen up," Max said and then continued. "Your biggest problem is and always has been your buddy, Dawson. There's still time for you to get your shit straight. You don't have a whole lot of time left in country. If you will promise me to try your damn best to act like a proper Marine, I'll let you take your R&R and I won't proceed with the court martial; but, if you fuck up one more time, you'll spend the rest of this fucking war in the brig. Do you read me?"

"Yes Sir. I'll do my best, Sir."

"Good."

"What about Donnie, uh, Private Dawson I mean?"

"What about him?" Max asked.

"Is he going to be court martialed for the pot?"

"Leave that to me and just concern yourself with PFC Corbett."

"Yes, Sir."

"By the way Corbett, where are you going on R&R?"

"Australia, Sir."

Just the sound of the word made his heart throb. He wanted desperately to see Amber again.

"Hey, Corbett, what did the Lieutenant want?" Dawson questioned as he watched Corbett walk away from the Lieutenant.

"He said you're a big fuckup and I should get my shit together, that's all."

"Oh yeah, what about your R&R?"

"He's letting me go," Corbett said.

"Good"

"What are you up to, Donnie?"

"Don't sweat it."

With the sun out a few days, the water inside the PPB had dried up and the Huey was able to land and pick up the tents and extra ammo crates. The platoon, however, was to hump back to the road and would be picked up by six-bys, sometime. They got to the road, spread out and rested for about an hour. With no sign of the trucks, Max had the platoon spread out along both sides of the road and they headed north towards Danang on foot rather than remaining stationary and allowing themselves to be targeted by enemy rockets or mortars.

The next day back at Battalion, Max handed Corbett a letter addressed to an address in Australia. "Listen, I want you to do me a favor and mail this letter immediately once you get to Sydney, okay? If I mail it from here, it will take twice as long to get there."

"Sure, Lieutenant," Corbett said.

Dawson approached Corbett as Corbett packed. "What do you have there?"

"The Lieutenant gave me a letter to mail."

"Let me see it."

"Now Donnie, I told the Lieutenant I would mail it for him."

"I'll take that letter. Now you take this one and mail it, you hear?"

"I don't want to get in no more trouble with the Lieutenant, Donnie."

"We're just going to have a little fun, that's all… just a little fun. Now don't worry and don't mention a word of this to anyone."

"Okay, but what are you gonna do with the Lieutenant's letter?"

"I'll handle it. Now pack your shit and go get laid."

Corbett left for the R&R center in Danang and when no one else was around, Dawson opened the Lieutenant's letter addressed to Miss Amber McEwen and read it before he burned it.

Dear Amber,

I'm beginning to feel like a short-timer. With only forty-two days left in country I find it difficult to think about anything but you. I hope this letter finds you and Amy both well and happy.

The war's the same. Nothing ever changes except more people die on both sides and the destruction of villages, displacing people from homes their families occupied for centuries, continues. Sometimes I really try hard to understand our reason for being here. Yesterday we even killed a water buffalo. Enough about Vietnam.

I'll bet Amy is walking all over the place by now. How is she? Any new teeth? Are things still going well at the shop?

Have you been in touch with your Mom and brother? Please send them my best the next time you speak to them. Amber, have you given any more thought about moving home? Personally, I think it would be good for you.

I've been thinking. When I get back to the States in July, I have thirty days leave before my next assignment. I want you to come to the U.S. then. I'll send airline tickets for the both of you.

The Skipper has sent for me so I have to close for now. I miss you both terribly.

All my love,

Max

"Ain't that just real cute", Dawson thought to himself as he dropped the burning paper.

Kilo Company would have it easy for the next couple of weeks, conducting several local day patrols but otherwise doing nothing more than providing perimeter security for the Battalion. Max finished reading "Exodus" and then read a Louis L'Amour western he'd found in the "four-holer." The slack time also gave him an opportunity to catch up on some letter writing to family and friends back home. All the while his thoughts kept returning to the girl down under who haunted his heart. He delayed writing another letter to Amber until he received her next letter, which he expected any day.

A letter from Australia did arrive two days later, but it wasn't in her handwriting.

Dear Max,

I'm afraid this letter brings you bad news, so I'll make it brief. A tragic accident occurred last week. Amber was crossing a street and was struck by an on-coming car. She was rushed to the hospital but never regained consciousness. She died the next day. There is nothing more I can say, except that I know she loved you.

Oli

Max read the letter over and over again, each time not believing what his eyes were telling him. He began to shake, and for the first time since that night alone in the foxhole, he cried. There were no other officers in the hooch at the time and although he wanted to cry out loud for the pain he felt, he cried silently while his body trembled and his heart shattered.

Operation Pipestone Canyon would be his sixth and last major combat operation before heading home. Captain Pete Mitchell completed his tour and already left Vietnam. Max, a First lieutenant, was given the job of Company Commander, normally a captain's billet. While the added responsibilities imposed upon him occupied his mind, he felt a huge emptiness within and really no longer cared if he lived or died. A few times while under fire on the operation he exposed himself to enemy fire and luckily escaped harm. He thought only of Amber and the life he envisioned they would someday share together- now dead. He thought of the baby, Amy, who would now most likely be raised by her grandmother, Delia.

It took him some time to find the right moment to write a letter to Delia and John. When that time came, he poured his heart out to them, expressing his condolences for their loss as well as his deep sadness over what could have been. He had loved their daughter and sister and would mourn her loss indefinitely. Placing the letter in a large sack of outgoing mail to be tossed on the next chopper, he turned his attentions back to his job, that of commanding Kilo Company during the final push of Pipestone Canyon.

When the company returned to Battalion after the thirty-day operation, he learned the final tally of both friendly and enemy KIA and WIA as well as captured enemy soldiers and weapons. He also learned of Marine Corps losses in equipment. Those items included one Marine Corps CH-46 helicopter shot down with the loss of all seven Marines on board. In yet another sad twist of fate, Max would not know that on board that chopper which had crashed and burned was, among other things, an outgoing mailbag.

The day finally came when Max Elliot was to leave Vietnam. The day he dreamed would never come had arrived, thirteen long months to the day, yet he felt no celebration. He even contemplated extending his tour another six months.

Realizing that extending his tour was only a subconscious death wish, he came to his senses and chose to leave. As he boarded the World Airways chartered jet he stopped in the doorway and turned, looking back on the country one last time. How he survived or why he survived, he didn't know.

In the end, of the forty-five infantry officers from his OCS class in Quantico, twenty eight had been killed, sixteen during their first two months in Nam. Eleven others had been wounded, some quite seriously. Lt. Rick Foster, married with a child, was sent home a double amputee. The land mine that claimed his legs had taken one of his testicles, his left hand and one eye as well. Yet, selfishly perhaps, Max felt his greatest sadness at the loss of a girl he met in Australia...a girl who entered his heart and his life...a girl he loved who added saneness and humanity to an otherwise insane and inhumane war...a girl who offered hope for a future...a girl whose own future was turned around and made brighter by their encounter...a girl who no longer lived.

After a three-day stopover in Okinawa, the flight home resumed. He changed planes in California, going from a military flight from Okinawa to an American Airlines flight to Newark, New Jersey. He was met by his parents and other family members and then drove an hour south to his parent's home. He was exceptionally quiet in the car. The smell of the industrial city of Newark nauseated him. Talk bothered him.

He tried to be polite and answer questions from his family, but he really didn't feel much like talking. It was July 20,1969, the day Neil Armstrong walked on the moon. Max sat before the TV set in his parent's living room and watched the live broadcast. "One small step for man, one giant leap for mankind." He was perplexed. *How the hell can we solve such conceivably insurmountable problems and land a man on the moon, yet we still solve out political problems by killing each other?*

He spent the next few weeks mostly at the beach. He stared at the ocean as if looking for answers...but to what? At night he found himself in bars drinking. While others drank to have a good time, Max drank to drown his sorrow.

After thirty days leave, he reported to Camp Lejeune, North Carolina, for his next duty assignment which would last until he completed his Marine Corps obligation in another ten months. Up until the week he was to be released from active duty he had no idea what he was going to do with his life or where he would go.

One night while sitting at the bar in the Officer's Club at Lejeune, he met another officer who suggested he go to Boston.

"What's in Boston?" Max questioned.

"You kidding?" he said. "Boston's a great city! Lots going on. And women? Wow! Do you know there are seventeen degree-granting institutions in Boston?" And the captain went on and on about all the splendid virtues of Boston. Max remembered the late Bill Cranston, the cocky Harvard grad who was killed shortly after taking command of the Third platoon. Bill had loved Boston.

For lack of any other direction, Max loaded his '67 Firebird convertible and drove north.

CHAPTER 14

Boston

There were perhaps fifty other applicants for the administrative assistant job at the Boston Gas Company. The personnel director, Bob Givens, did the interviewing and hiring. He was a retired military man. Max got the job over many other applicants, most of who were just out of college. There is a fraternity, of sorts, among military men, particularly war veterans.

Bob Givens and Max Elliot both were cognizant of its existence during Max's interviews prior to being hired, yet neither man mentioned it. Perhaps he would have landed the job on his own merit, but membership in the elusive fraternity clinched it.

Having been a military "professional," Max was accustomed to taking orders as well as giving them, and in either case, following through to see that the job was done effectively. But in civilian life, things were different. He had no one to give orders to, not even a secretary. There was a secretarial pool and he found himself politely begging a secretary when he needed something done.

When he went to his boss to suggest a more efficient way of getting a task accomplished or to point out an area of waste and inefficiency, he was told not to "rock the boat."

The gas company's profits are regulated by the Department of Public Utilities," his boss said, "thereby what isn't paid out in salaries is paid in taxes." As such, the company payroll carried an exorbitant amount of "dead weight."

When Max went to another member of higher management and told him he needed more work and responsibilities, he was told to "take it easy." His only real work occurred once a month when he was to complete a budget variance report, explaining why actual expenditures differed from the budget forecast.

In one report, he truthfully reported a legal settlement with a customer. He was given the report back and told to change it to falsely show an "outside engineering study," which would make the level of management above him look better to their superiors on the Board of Directors.

Max had a difficult time. He still loved and mourned Amber and Amy. He hated his civilian job, considering it the most boring thing he had ever done.

At Camp Lejeune, then at the rank of captain, he was the company commander of Lima Company, Third Battalion, Eighth Marines. After a couple months on the job at the gas company, he found himself going to lunch at the Playboy Club almost daily and not coming back to work until four or four thirty in the afternoon and then going home at five.

Often times, he was too drunk to even go back, so he went straight home or elsewhere after leaving the Playboy Club. What made matters worse, was when his conscience bothered him and he told his boss exactly what he was doing, the boss didn't care since most of his salesmen where likewise sandbagging time.

What was a gas salesman suppose to do when he didn't have any surplus gas to sell? Cryogenic carriers, ships that could transport liquefied natural gas from Algiers to Massachusetts were just coming into being but the gas company had only one storage facility built which could hold the temperature to below minus 260 degrees Fahrenheit thereby maintaining the gas in the liquefied state where it occupied 1/600th the volume it would otherwise require in the gaseous state. The gas company was essentially in a holding pattern.

Max drank more and more. Most nights would find him in a bar. One night he frequented a bar in Cambridge which was located in a cellar, much like the Rathskeller in Kings Cross. He sat at the bar and drank beer, lots of beer. Two rough-looking men of substantial size, probably longshoremen, were also at the bar. They were loud and obnoxious.

Max was sitting quietly, drowning his sorrows deeper with each Budweiser. The raucous dockworkers were already getting on his nerves when one of them provoked him. Max told him to "fuck off," and that appeared to be the end of it. When he finally staggered out of the bar perhaps ten or fifteen minutes after the other two had left he was quite drunk. He had no sooner walked out the door that closed behind him when he was kicked in his face by the larger of the two men who stood by the railing along the stairwell. Max never saw the kick coming.

Nor did he have much recollection of the subsequent beating he took when the two men jumped him in the stairwell and punched and kicked him into unconsciousness. By the time the police arrived, his attackers were gone. The white towel the proprietor of the bar gave him ran red with blood absorbed from various lacerations and bruises around his face and mouth.

He met and dated several girls during those months in Boston, but he measured them all against Amber and none compared. He met a girl, a pre-law student at Northeastern. She was attractive and he was even enjoying her company until the topic of conversation shifted to Vietnam.

Boston was active with anti-war sentiments. The Pentagon Papers had recently been released. Before long, their conversation, which he tried to avoid and she pursued, turned ugly and she stormed out of the bar—but not before calling him a "baby killer."

Perhaps he was...how many of the charred remains from the napalm strikes were babies? But he was pinned down in the rice paddies...they started shooting first...what was he to do? Was he to carry guilt for the remainder of his life? No matter what pretty name the media wanted to give it, it was war...war is ugly...war is death, destruction, devastation, inhumanity and purpose...purpose?

He'd supported his government...he'd served his country...shouldn't he feel pride instead of shame? He had to re-think the purpose. His thoughts and emotions became ambivalent.

And so it went. Max was in a big city when he hated cities; in a blasé job when he wanted and needed meaning; and had a social life that consisted of heavy drinking and altercations. He found it best to avoid any mention of the Corps and Vietnam just to avoid arguments.

One cold winter day as he aimlessly slogged thru the slush along a downtown street while the sleet continued to fall, his eyes captured a Marlboro cigarette advertisement on a large billboard. The cowboy smoking the Marlboro sat upon a sorrel steed, the shearling lining of his suede coat and the Silverbelly Stetson upon his head transcended Max's mind to another place.

The cowboy held the lead rope of a grey he ponied, while beyond the rangy aspens loomed the snow-capped Rockies. The noxious fumes of a bus filled the air and as it passed, its right front wheel hit the pothole and the mud and freezing slush ran down his trenchcoat. He was still staring at the billboard when the panhandler, adorned with peace symbols, approached.

"Hey man, could you spare some change?"

Max moved his eyes from the billboard where he was steadfast in thought and looked at the man, at first not saying anything. "Get a fucking job," he asserted with disdain. The panhandler cowed and grumbled inaudible sounds as he retreated.

The next day he quit his job at the gas company, packed the Firebird, and left his apartment and the city he'd never assimilated into. Heading west, he drove aimlessly…a drifter with no destination other than a direction that followed the setting sun. He was glad to be out of Boston, the belly of liberalism. He searched desperately to find meaning to his life.

If only Amber were still alive he thought over and over again. "Maybe I should have stayed in the Corps?" he thought at times, then usually reversed that thought realizing he would have gone back to Vietnam for another thirteen months. He no longer wanted to play the game of kill or be killed. He had enough of that.

In southwest Colorado just before the continental divide, he found a small town with a population of only about four-hundred permanent residents nestled in a valley between the Sangre de Cristo range and the Wet Mountains. He rented a small cabin on the mountainside, and traded the Firebird in on a four-wheel drive vehicle needed to reach the cabin.

The used jeep reminded him of their drive to the Sunrise, when Oli loaned them her jeep; when Amber sat beside him and Amy cackled in the back. As he drove up the rarely traveled unpaved and challenging mountain road he looked to the empty seat beside him and created a vision of the dark haired, green eyed beauty, whose image was as natural as the ponderosa and pinion pine, as wholesome as all nature around him and more loving than the doe nuzzling her fawn among the aspen in the snow by the stream.

The cabin likewise elicited memories. He was reminded of the line shack by the precipice overlooking the valley where the stock wintered along the meandering river...where they made love while the warm breezes sang their song as the horses grazed in the paddock.

But Amber was no more. The wood stove was not unlike the stove in the line shack on the other side of the world in a place down under. It was cold in the mountains this time of year, and he spent his days chopping wood, reading and occasionally going into town to shop for groceries and other needed items. And every day when the dawn showered amber rays of light across the eastern sky, he missed her.

* * * * *

In the spring came a job offer at the dude ranch nestled on the east slope of the Sangres. Max was hired as a wrangler, doing odd jobs around the ranch and once he learned the mountain trails, taking guests on trail rides into the mountains where the bear and mule deer and the eagles were free.

He thought of another trail ride a time ago when the koala bears dallied in the trees and the kangaroo cavorted on the trail ahead...when his horse stumbled and fell and Amber rushed to his side thinking he was hurt...

when he pulled her to the ground and ran his fingers thru her satiny hair as he kissed her delicious lips. At last he was content. At least as content as he could be when his heart was torn. He would be content, for a while at least.

* * * * * *

Phil Renfro, now Captain Renfro, was a lifer. He didn't care much for the stateside Corps after returning from Nam so when he got his orders for his second tour, he was pleased. Phil was an adventurer. Single, he liked to live life on the edge. The night he and Max sat up in the tent in the platoon patrol base near Thai Cam he went on and on telling Max about how much he loved to race his motorcycle and sky dive, while the monsoon rains pelted the canvas above.

Phil was now taking his R&R in Sydney. During his first tour in Nam he went to Bangkok where he "bought" an Asian companion for the week, or so he told Max that night in the tent above the tumultuous roar of the rain.

In Kings Cross not much had changed over the past year. The Vietnam War continued, so soldiers came and went on R&R, romances developed, hearts were sometimes broken and the merchants and the prostitutes prospered. Phil was walking the streets of Kings Cross when the tall, slender woman, about twenty- four or twenty-five years old, with short black hair and large dark brown eyes, approached him. She had a chiseled look about her, but yet, like a store window mannequin, was attractive.

"Do you want to go?" she said.

It was said Phil Renfro would do it to a snake if you held it down, so accepting this young woman's solicitation was not a difficult choice. After all, the woman he kept in Bangkok he paid for an entire week. "Sure honey, let's boogey."

As they walked down the street towards the place on the second floor where Mr. Wimple still made his weekly visits and GI's and others paid their dues for services rendered, the girl made small talk. "So what are you in, army, navy or what?" she asked.

"Neither," Phil replied. "Marine Corps."

"Are you an officer?" she asked.

"Yeah, why do you ask? Do officers get a discount or do they pay a premium?"

"Same price," she said as she ambled along, her high heels occasionally dragging on the sidewalk because her mini-skirt was so tight she couldn't lift her feet high enough. "It's just that I once knew a Marine officer, a lieutenant, real nice guy. My girlfriend was madly in love with him. What a shame."

"What happened?" Phil asked as they turned the corner.

"Got himself killed in Nam. Broke my friend's heart. It's still broken. She can't forget the guy and go on with her life."

"That's too bad," Phil said. "A lot of Marine lieutenants didn't make it through Nam."

"Hey, maybe you knew this guy. His name was Max, uh, Max Elliot."

"Max Elliot! Lieutenant Max Elliot, USMC?"

"Yeah, did you know him?"

"Honey, your girlfriend's name wouldn't happen to be Amber, would it?"

"How'd you know that?"

"Sweetheart, Max Elliot ain't dead! He talked my ear off one night in Nam as we sat in a tent trying to keep our feet dry. All he talked about was this girl in Australia named Amber whom he was madly in love with. He's as alive as you and me this minute, or at least he was when I last saw him at Lejeune."

"You mean he wasn't killed in Vietnam? Max is alive?"

"Yeah, I just told you he was alive!"

"Yikes!" Oli screamed. She grabbed Phil's head with both hands and pulled it towards her, planting a big kiss on his cheek, just as they reached the doorway to the brothel. "Where is he now?" she asked excitedly.

"Don't know. When I last saw him at Lejeune he was getting out of the Corps. Said something about maybe going to Boston, but that's all I know."

"I got to go!" she said as she started running down the street, stopping momentarily to take off her shoes so she could run faster.

"What about us?" Phil shouted.

"Later, and it will be a freebee!"

"What's your name?" Phil once again shouted as the girl ran down the street.

"Oli," she replied.

CHAPTER 15

The Search

Even in June, the air was cool at the higher elevations. The peaks of the Sangres remained snow capped through most of the summer. Max felt better in the mountains which loomed to fourteen-thousand feet as they poked through the clouds and trailed their way to Santa Fe.

He got along well with the other wranglers, mostly men from Colorado, Wyoming and Montana who grew up on ranches and were real cowboys. But Max held his own amongst his peers.

He had certainly seen far more of the world and experienced more than the others, even the older men, and they sensed a certain difference about him. But Max remained fairly quiet about himself and while the others knew he had served in Vietnam, they knew little else, as it was a subject Max preferred to avoid.

In his wallet he carried a picture of himself and Amber, taken on the sand at Bondi Beach. He could feel the warmth of the sun and the smell of the salt air blended with the smell of the suntan oil that glowed on her bronzed skin. And he could always smell her hair and the musk perfume… all that and more, just from looking at the picture.

He began to feel at peace with himself, healing from the war. He would occasionally wake up from his sleep in a nightmare. His worst and most frequent nightmare was of a boy and an old man with horrible napalm burns who jeered at him as they passed by him, the boy's skin sloughing off until all that remained was a skeleton with two hollow eye sockets.

But he had pleasant dreams as well. Dreams about his time with Amber, only to awaken to a reality less tender than the dream and always leaving him depressed.

His favorite times were taking ranch guests on trail rides into higher elevations. The ranch was nestled in the foothills near the valley floor, itself a high mountain plateau nearing eight-thousand feet above sea level. Yet the summer temperature was in the eighties with no humidity.

Riding the horses slowly up the winding paths to the tree line at ten to eleven-thousand feet you could look out at the valley floor below from breaks in the timber. It was an awesome sight, even more spectacular from a position upon a stout horse standing in a foot of snow surrounded by temperatures twenty degrees less than that being viewed. In the fertile valley below, green pastures painted with wild flowers contrasted with the ponderosa pines and the white bark of the aspen in the foothills. Looking about at those views, Max felt insignificant in the realm of nature…a mere snowflake among the snow capped peaks of the mountain range, a single blade of grass in the valley floor or a pebble on a granite precipice piercing the clouds. It was that perspective, that serenity that kept Max Elliot alive and nurtured.

* * * * * *

"Boston? How am I going to find him in Boston, Oli? I know, I'll go there, that's it."

"Hold on a minute," Oli said with a sigh, "let's give this some thought first before you start traveling half way around the world."

"The telephone! That's it," Amber cried. "He must have a telephone in Boston. How do I get information in Boston?"

"Here, give me the phone. I once had to get assistance to track down a company in Chicago that made some stupid mining equipment that Robert needed for his stupid opal mine."

Oli got through to directory assistance in Boston, Massachusetts. "Yes operator, I'm trying to get the number for a Max Elliot, that's with two L's and one T. Yes, I'll hold, thank you." She smiled at Amber. "She's looking it up." Amber was so nervous she gnawed on her fingernails.

The operator came back. Oli covered the receiver with her palm and turned to Amber. "That number has been disconnected." She listened again.

"But you must have a new number," Oli protested.

She listened another moment and then hung up the phone.

"I'm sorry, there was no other listing under that name," Oli whispered.

"I'm going to Boston," Amber said.

Oli shook her head and put a hand on Amber's shoulder. "Slow down child, we'll find him."

"We'll hire a private investigator, that's it. A private investigator will find him."

"Okay, great idea. How many private investigators do you know in Boston?"

"None," Amber responded sadly.

"Hey, I got an idea. I know a bloke who does that sort of thing here in Sydney. Maybe he can connect us with someone in Boston."

Oli phoned her friend, Bruce Watson, who ran a one-man investigative service he called "Four-Eyes." Oli didn't want to tell Amber, but she felt the eccentric Mr. Watson probably couldn't find his own brother in a room full of Chinamen, yet maybe he *could* help out in some way. Amber stood holding her breath as Oli made the call.

"Yes Bruce, thank you. Please call as soon as possible. Yes Bruce, thank you, Bruce. We'll be waiting by the phone."

Oli put down the receiver and turned to Amber. "It's the middle of the night in Boston. Bruce will call first thing when it's morning there and then call us. He'll find Max, I know he will." Oli placed her arm around Amber's shoulder to reassure her.

"I can't believe it, he's really alive. Why did he stop writing? I wonder if he was hurt? Maybe he didn't remember us! I don't understand. Why that letter? What's going on, Oli?"

"I don't know either, honey, but we are going to find out as soon as we find Max."

Amber watched the clock that seemed to move slower than ever before. The evening dragged on but she never left the phone. It was almost 2 a.m. when she was awakened by the ringing as she slept on the sofa.

"I'm sorry to call at this dreadful hour," Bruce said, "but Oli said the matter was quite urgent."

"Yes, it is. Thank you, I'm Amber. I've been waiting by the phone for your call. Did you find him? Did you find Max Elliot?"

"Not exactly, but I located a colleague I once met in the States, a retired FBI agent. He lives in Boston. It's about 11 AM yesterday in Boston now. Strange, isn't it? Us being a day ahead of them, that is."

Amber didn't care what time it was anywhere. "What about finding Max? Will he do it?"

"Yes, yes, he'll do it for a nominal amount plus expenses."

"I don't care, just please find him. And quickly!"

"He's already working on it. I'll call you as soon as I learn something. Cheers!" And he hung up.

Oli rubbed the sleep from her eyes as she walked from her bedroom. "How'd old Bruce do?"

"He said he has some FBI agent working on it. He'll call us when he learns something. Did the phone wake Amy?"

"I don't think so."

Oli and Amber sat up talking for almost an hour as they sipped honey laced tea. Amber fell back to sleep on the sofa when she was once again awakened by the phone.

"Four-Eyes at your service," he said.

"Did you find Max?"

"Not exactly. Seems he worked for the gas company for a spell, then up and left. No one knows where he went. He just quit his job and left."

"But he must be in Boston somewhere?" Amber said anxiously.

"I don't think so. My friend talked to some chap at the gas company who seemed to know Mr. Elliot the best. He said Max told him he was leaving Boston and going west."

"West where? Did he say where he was going?"

"No, just that he was going out west. I am truly sorry, but we haven't given up. I'm sure we will find this Max Elliot somewhere."

"Thank you, Mr. Watson."

Amber hung up the phone, put down her head and wept.

* * * * * *

Autumn came early in the Rocky Mountains. Snow closed the trails and the dude ranch braced for the winter weather storing tons of rich, green, sweet smelling alfalfa hay. Most of the wranglers headed home to tend to their own spreads for the winter months but a few remained. The guests stopped coming, going instead to the ski resort areas of Colorado, such as Vail, Aspen and Telluride.

"You're sure welcome to winter here, Max," said Gary Stevens, who along with his wife Liz, owned and managed the ranch.

Gary had met Liz back east eleven years prior and after they married he moved her to the ranch that he had inherited from his parents. Liz was from New York but wouldn't trade her life on the ranch for the city at any price.

Max could easily identify with that. "Thanks, Gary. I really do appreciate the offer, but I need to move on. Got something I have to do. Perhaps you can use me again come next spring?"

"Anytime you want, you've got a job and a home here," Gary said.

"We mean it, too." Liz interjected. "We're going to miss you."

"Thank you both very much. It's been a real pleasure. If it's okay, I'll be leaving in the morning after I feed the horses."

"No need to bother. I'll do the feeding," Gary said. "Get yourself an early start if you like."

"Not before breakfast!" Liz insisted. "I'll have Tully fix us steak and eggs tomorrow. A real going away breakfast!"

"That's great," Max said. "I'll see you for breakfast then."

After breakfast and goodbyes, Max drove the red jeep to Denver, about a three and a half hour drive. The second car dealer gave him the better price and he took it. Forty-five hundred dollars cash would be more than enough to pay for the plane ticket. He grabbed his jacket and his old Marine Corps duffle bag from the back of the jeep and took a room at the airport Marriott for the night. His plane would leave in the morning.

* * * * * *

When Bruce Watson didn't call her, Amber called him. It was nine days later before anything was learned.

"He went to Colorado. The Division of Motor Vehicles there said he traded in one car for another."

"Do you have a phone number or address for him?" Amber asked.

"He never had a phone there. We did get an address for him, but he checked out of there just a few days ago. We just missed him."

"What about a job? Does he work in Colorado?"

"My contact in Boston said that he traced Mr. Elliot to a dude ranch where he worked. But again, he left that place a few days ago. The proprietor, a Mr. Stevens, said that your Mr. Elliot said he had to move on. Didn't say where he was going and Mr. Steven's felt he would be intruding to ask. Seems Mr. Elliot would have volunteered his destination had he wanted to. Sounded as though Mr. Elliot was planning to return in the spring, though. "

"Anything else?"

"Not now, I'll let you know."

"Thank you, Mr. Watson."

* * * * * *

Cruising over the Pacific at thirty-eight-thousand feet, Max stared out the window at the clouds below, occasionally getting a glimpse of the sea through breaks in the cloud cover. The sea reflected the sun and shimmered in the light. It seemed so flat and calm at this altitude. Max wondered if in fact it was really rough with seas of ten feet or more. He couldn't tell from this altitude.

He thought about the last time he flew. It was his return home from Vietnam. That was after he learned of Amber's death. He thought about his last flight back from Sydney. That was a good flight. He was so in love. He didn't think much during that flight of the war he was going back to. He thought mostly of the girl he was leaving behind. He thought about their future after the war, the future that would not be.

For hours Max stared at the clouds, at the sea and at the horizon. Lost in his memories he replayed those precious moments they had spent together. He clearly envisioned the moment when he first laid eyes on her on the sidewalk in Kings Cross. He remembered how he was enamored by her even then.

He thought about little Amy. Once before he left Sydney the last time she had called him "Daddy." What does a child know? She wasn't his child, but he could have been her father. He wanted to be her father. What was to become of sweet, precious, little Amy McEwen?

* * * * * *

"Miss McEwen?"

"Yes, this is she."

"Bruce Watson, once again at your service."

"Yes, Mr. Watson, what have you learned?"

Watson paused as if reluctant to go on. Amber sensed his uneasiness even over the telephone. "Mr. Elliot sold his car in Denver. He didn't trade it for another, so Motor Vehicles has no current address for him. I'm afraid we have reached a dead end for the moment."

Amber slowly hung up the phone. Despondency filled her heart. She took Amy for a walk but was saddened throughout the remainder of the day.

Later that evening she broke the news to Oli. "I'm going home. Amy and I will take the bus in the morning."

"I understand. You'll probably be happier, your mother and all."

Amber shook her head, not bothering to stop the tears that trickled down her face. "He disappeared. We were so close to finding him and he just disappeared."

"Listen, I'll call you just as soon as Bruce finds something. Cheer up, will you? He's alive and we'll find him, okay?"

It was difficult, but Amber worked up a smile. She gave Oli a hug. "You're the best friend anyone could ever have. Thank you for being here for me."

"Yeah, me too. I feel the same way. Now let's get you and Amy packed before I start to cry.

CHAPTER 16

The Sunrise

The "no smoking" and "fasten your seatbelt" signs illuminated concurrently with the sound of the chimes. A few moments later the flight attendant made her announcement, Max felt his ears pop as the aircraft descended.

He wasn't sure why he was flying halfway around the world. Perhaps he wasn't ready to let go of his memories just yet. He wanted to find out what he could of Amber's last days before the accident. He wanted to visit her grave- to be near her for the last time. And he wanted to see Amy and to pay his respects to Amber's family. It was long past time for that, but he hadn't been able to do it before although he wondered at times why they didn't answer his condolence letter he wrote from Nam. Perhaps they misplaced his address or lost track of him after he returned to the States.

It was for these reasons alone that he traveled the distance. He didn't know how long he would remain in Australia. He might stay only a few days, a week, or longer.

This time he would not be renting his clothes at the Chevron Hotel. The duffle bag contained all he needed. He took a cab from the airport and instructed the cabbie to deliver him to the bungalow Amber shared with Oli. At least that was his initial intention.

"Driver, I've changed my mind. Drop me in Kings Cross." He got out in front of the Chevron and slung the strap of the duffle bag over his shoulder. He did not go into the hotel but stood and watched as others entered and left. Most were obviously American servicemen on R&R. He began to walk. Another GI walked arm in arm with a pretty blond. He was glad that at least he would not have to go back to the war. The GI would. He didn't envy him. The war, while winding down, was still on.

While back in Colorado winter winds chilled the air, summer was coming to the Continent. The walk felt good after the long plane ride. He stopped occasionally to rest. The duffle was heavy. He really didn't expect anyone to be home when he knocked on the door. The screen door didn't close all the way so when he knocked the whole door banged against the jam. It was Oli who answered.

"My God, it's you!" she exclaimed with astonishment.

"Hello, Oli, how are you?" Max said as he gave her a hug. "You're looking good."

Oli's jaw dropped. She was speechless. She did not know how to say it. "We tried to find you. We hired an investigator."

"Why were you trying to find me?"

Oli's heart raced. "The letter. It said you were dead."

Max carefully gripped Oli's shoulders. "What are you talking about?"

"The letter. Amber got a letter from some sergeant. Said you were killed. Then this other lieutenant I met, knew you. He said you *weren't* dead. We've been trying to find you."

"Oli, what do you mean by *we*?"

"Amber and I, who do you think?"

"What about the accident?" he asked.

"What accident?"

"Oli, are you saying Amber didn't have an accident? She's alive?"

"I don't know what's going on here. Of *course* she's alive!"

His head raced. His eyes overflowed with tears of happiness. His heart was about to jump from his body. "Where is she?" he asked excitedly.

"She went home...to the Sunrise."

Instinctively, Oli reached for the keys to her jeep, which were on the table. "Take it."

Max accepted the keys and gave Oli a near bone-crunching hug. "Oli, don't call her before I get there, okay?"

"Okay," she replied. As Max turned to leave, Oli picked up the letter and handed it to him. Why they'd kept it, she wasn't sure. Perhaps by re-reading it enough times it would go away...make things right...make him not dead.

"This is the letter she got."

He looked at it. "Dawson. Fucking Dawson! It had to be."

"Who is Dawson?" she asked.

Max was steaming. The stationary was identical to that of the letter he received allegedly from Oli. So was the handwriting.

"He was a shit-bird Marine in Nam. I had him court-martialed for smoking dope among other things. He sent me a letter saying Amber had a fatal accident." Max pondered. "But the letter I got was postmarked Sydney and Dawson never came here." He thought a brief moment longer.

"Damn! Why didn't I think of that before? Corbett! He had Corbett mail the letter when he went on R&R. And I gave him a letter to Amber to mail when he got here so she would get it sooner. She must not have gotten it."

"After the letter you're holding, she never got any others."

"I'll get the jeep back in a few days. And Oli, thanks."

"Just go already. I'm so damn happy myself I'm going to pee in my pants!"

It was getting late, almost midnight, but he wanted to cover as many miles as he could. Driving south almost as fast as the four-cylinder would go, Max was jubilant.

For the first time in a little over a year he felt alive! His senses rejuvenated. He unzipped the plastic window and let the chilly air in. It was chilly, but invigorating.

The air smelled wonderful. He couldn't remember air ever smelling so delicious. He could barely hear anything above the pitch of the max-revved engine, the rapid fluttering of the soft top, and the roar of the wind. He sang anyway.

"It's knowing that your door is always open and your path is free to walk...." He knew many but not all of words to the popular Glen Campbell song. It didn't matter. He could barely hear himself anyway.

Through the night he drove. As dawn broke he pulled into a station and gassed up and grabbed a cup of coffee to go. As he jumped back into the jeep he looked at the eastern sky. "An amber dawn", he whispered, "and what a beautiful dawn it is... only about seventy more miles to go".

John McEwen was outside the barn when Max drove up.

"Max! By God, it's good to see you! We thought you was a goner!"

"Good to see you too, John. Where is she?"

"She didn't know you were coming, mate—thought you were dead— then learned you weren't. She got an early start. Left almost an hour ago. Rode out to the old line-shack. You know how to get there, don't you?"

"Yeah, but that country is too rough even for this jeep. Can I take a horse, John?"

"Take mine, he's already saddled."

"Thanks." Max mounted, reined the horse around, clucked, then squeezed his leg into the sorrel's side breaking into a cantor almost immediately. He maintained a steady pace dodging the occasional wombat burrow and acacia.

The gelding wanted to run, but Max held his speed not wanting to use him up before he reached the shack. At a small creek, the sorrel hesitated then leaped across. Max was nearly unseated, not expecting the horse to jump the water, but he supported himself on the horse's neck upon landing and resumed stride.

He spied the shack. Tuffy was grazing in the paddock. He dismounted and loosely wrapped the reins over the log top-rail. It was windy on the hilltop and she didn't hear him ride up. But there she was, sitting on a large boulder by the precipice overlooking the valley below. Her long dark hair blew in the wind. As he approached from fifteen yards the bay whinnied. Amber turned and saw him. She rose suddenly, took a step forward, then stopped.

Max could see the tears already halfway down her cheeks. Her green eyes glistened. He walked slowly towards her and she to him. At five paces she ran into his arms.

Max held her tightly, his face nestled into her neck and hair. She was sobbing his name as he was whispering hers while his tears also fell. Their heads parted and he held her face. He kissed her tears, then her lips.

"I love you so much," she cried.

"And I love you," he said. He held her firmly again. "I see you haven't done much to fix up our homestead," Max said jokingly as he nodded towards the shack.

Amber managed a brief chuckle and wiped her eyes. Max kissed her again, long and gentle, then picked her up and carried her across the threshold.

This time the sorrel whinnied while the wind sang as two became one. The arduous journey from Vietnam to Sunrise is complete.

Made in the USA
Middletown, DE
03 December 2015